"What does it mean to hit a home run?" asked Ava

"To hit a home run," Ian replied, his lips lowering to her collarbone.

"What does it mean with a woman? With me?"

Ian stopped. Glanced at her. "To make love to you."

Her body trembled. She was ready for a home run. "Ian, would you like to come up to my apartment for some coffee?"

"I can't tell you how much I'd love a cup of coffee."

It was the quickest she'd ever exited a car. He followed her upstairs and into her apartment, nothing and no one around them. They were the only two people in the world. The large front room was still scented with the sexy subtle hints of massage oil.

Ian locked the door behind them and trailed her into the kitchen. "Should I actually pretend to make it?" she asked.

A smile briefly touched his lips as he practically stalked toward her. Ava sucked in a breath. The dating lessons had stopped. Now they were just man and woman. And primal instinct.

Blaze™

Dear Reader,

The best thing about being a writer is that I can have a taste of the careers I've missed out on. In *Tall, Dark and Filthy Rich* I learned all about being a private investigator. Next book might be rocket science. This book is anthropology.

Anthropology was one of my favorite subjects in school, just as it was Ava's. In fact, she's immersed herself so much into the dating and courtship rituals from other lands that she actually doesn't know a thing about how they're handled in her homeland.

That's where Ian Cole steps in!

I really enjoyed researching all these different customs, but I also threw in several of my own.

I love hearing from readers. You can contact me at jill@jillmonroebooks.com or visit my Web site at www.jillmonroe.com.

Jill

PRIMAL INSTINCTS
Jill Monroe

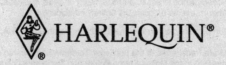

HARLEQUIN®

TORONTO • NEW YORK • LONDON
AMSTERDAM • PARIS • SYDNEY • HAMBURG
STOCKHOLM • ATHENS • TOKYO • MILAN • MADRID
PRAGUE • WARSAW • BUDAPEST • AUCKLAND

ISBN-13: 978-0-373-79382-2
ISBN-10:   0-373-79382-0

PRIMAL INSTINCTS

Copyright © 2008 by Jill Floyd.

Printed in U.S.A.

ABOUT THE AUTHOR

Jill Monroe makes her home in Oklahoma with her family. When not writing, she spends way too much time on the Internet completing "research" or updating her blog. Even when writing, she's thinking of ways to avoid cooking.

Books by Jill Monroe

HARLEQUIN BLAZE
245—SHARE THE DARKNESS
304—HITTING THE MARK
362—TALL, DARK AND FILTHY RICH

HARLEQUIN BLAZE
1003—NEVER NAUGHTY ENOUGH

Don't miss any of our special offers. Write to us at the following address for information on our newest releases.

Harlequin Reader Service
U.S.: 3010 Walden Ave., P.O. Box 1325, Buffalo, NY 14269
Canadian: P.O. Box 609, Fort Erie, Ont. L2A 5X3

As always, thanks go to my husband and family, who are always patient. I love you, Pink!

To Gnomey, may you someday find your way back to me. To Lobby, may the day come soon when I can give your brother to Gena. But never you. You I'm keeping.

Thanks always goes to Gena Showalter, Sheila Fields, Donnell Epperson, Kassia Krozser, and Betty Sanders. Kassia—I put the serial comma in there just for you.

To Jeff Z, my BFF and all my friends from PCHS—you rock!

1

Middle of Nowhere, Oklahoma

WHAT WAS SHE DOING? Or had just done? Miriam Cole
sucked in a breath and squeezed her eyes tight. It didn't
change a thing. *He* was still there.

Miriam peeked over her shoulder at the man smushed
up against her body. His legs were tangled over hers and
his hand gently gripped her breast. The angle was awkward, but she could make him out perfectly in the
morning light.

She sucked in a breath as she gazed at his sexy,
slightly curling dark hair. That full bottom lip that did
such dangerous things to her body. That face that looked
almost boyish in his sleep.

Boyish, because the man beside her was twenty years
old.

Twenty. Twenty? She had to get out of there.

How had this happened? Two days ago, getting a
rental and driving from Dallas to see a prospective
author in Oklahoma had seemed like such a great idea.
A couple of hours in the car with the top down. See a

part of the country she'd never seen before. Relax. Take a break.

But the clean air smelled weird, the wildflowers untamed, and after mentally going through her to-do list, she remembered why she hated time alone with herself. She had nothing but work on her mind.

When she returned to the office, she'd fire the person who'd suggested she take a vacation. Even if he was her brother.

The man beside her shifted and snuggled closer into her pillow, burying his face in her hair. She closed her eyes again, loving the feel of his skin against hers. Miriam began to curve her hand along the hardness of his biceps. Nothing felt as good as a man's strong arms. Jeremy's strong arms especially. Maybe a quick—

Her body jerked. Stop. If she went down that road again, he'd be awake. What had it been, four? Five times? Besides a little bit of sleep, the man didn't need much else to be up and raring to go. As tempting as round five or six sounded—escape was what she needed.

She slowly tugged her hair out from under him and slid gracelessly to the floor. He shifted, and she made every muscle in her body go still. She held her breath. After counting to ten, she slowly stood. Although way more prudent, she refused to crawl. Some dignity must be maintained. She was a major player in the publishing industry after all.

Oh, her brother Ian would laugh his head off if he knew she'd tiptoed naked to the bathroom. Brought down. Brought down by a temperamental sporty little red car and no bars on her cell phone. Stranded. Stranded somewhere in the middle of a place called Arbuckle Wilderness.

Her cell phone beeped and she dashed for it. No way did she want Jeremy waking up. He'd want to do something gallant like fix her breakfast or slay some kind of dragon.

"Hello?" she answered quickly.

That's when she realized that what she held in her hand wasn't her phone. What had seemed so funny the day before, that she and Jeremy had picked out the same built-in ring tone, now was another in an ever-growing list of events that had led her to the colossal mistake of falling into his arms last night.

The long pause on the other line was ended by a strangled throat clearing. "Who is this?" the woman demanded, her tone clearly not expecting any subterfuge.

Rather than answering, Miriam padded across the floor and shook Jeremy's shoulder. "Phone call for you," she told him as he opened his eyes and she met the blueness of his gaze, reminding her just why she'd kissed him that first time.

With a sexy shrug, he sat up in bed, the sheet slid down his legs. *Don't look.*

"Hello?" His voice sleepy and so appealing to her.

Oh, what did she have left to lose really? Her gaze drifted lower.

And Jeremy sat up straighter. "Oh, hi, Mom."

She shouldn't have looked.

She was going to be sick.

Two Weeks Later

"YOU LOOK LIKE HELL," Miriam said.

Ian Cole slumped into the burgundy leather chair in front of his editor's glass-and-chrome desk, ready for his latest assignment.

"That's a bit harsh," he told his sister.

"It's true. Have you seen yourself in the mirror?"

Maybe she had a point. He certainly felt like hell, and he probably looked it, too. Yeah, well, what else was new? "I've just spent three weeks tracking drug runners. You're lucky I caught a shower before catching the red-eye back to the States."

"Maybe you should try catching a shave and a hair-cut. And three days worth of sleep."

"The boys gave me a good send-off before I broke for the airport. A little R & R," he said, rubbing his temples, and trying to remember just what they'd done.

Maybe too good a send-off.

Miriam's lips thinned. "I'm not sure the parties those guys cook up could be cataloged as either rest or relaxation. They're certainly not good for you."

"We were all of legal age, and you didn't *have* to bail me out of jail, so I'm calling it good," he said, blinking against the light beaming through her large office window overlooking Manhattan.

Miriam shuddered, as she walked toward the window to close the blinds. "Thanks for the reminder. You should have heard me explaining to our accountant that bail money was a legitimate tax expense."

"You're lucky you got to bail me out. There are quite a few pissed-off officials who'd just as soon kill me as have me share the luxury of their penal system. There'll be no welcome mat for me in Mexico."

"True," his sister said, reaching for the wand on the blinds.

"Come to think of it, there'll be no welcome mat for you, either."

Miriam turned on her heel and glared at him. "You're right, and I have a time share in Mazatlan I'll never see again. I left my skinny swimsuit there, so screw your hangover. It's your own darn fault you're in this condition, so you can live with the sunlight. I like my view and I like my rays."

Ian looked around the office. "You worked hard enough to get here."

"Damn straight," she said, her angry attitude vanishing. He knew his big sister could never stay mad at him for long.

Kicking off her pointy black power heels, she rounded the corner of her desk. She tossed a manila folder on her brother's lap. "I have a new assignment for you. In fact, I think you'll like it. You've talked in the past about doing more feature writing, less field-work. I have a book for you to look over."

It physically hurt to make the face that expressed how he felt inside.

"You're going to tell me you're the only reporter who's never secretly longed to write their own book?" she asked.

"A book is a long way from a feature spread in a magazine."

"Think of it as one hundred features strung together. I need this to work. Cole Publishing has just acquired the rights to an exciting new concept book," she told him as she reached for her ever-present bottle of water.

Ian sat up in his chair. "Ah, the side trip to Oklahoma. I see it went down smoothly."

Miriam coughed on her water.

Expanding into books had been a dream of their father's, which he'd inherited from their grandfather, who'd founded Cole Publishing. They'd spun off a few books from their newsmagazine to other publishers in the past, but the dream of becoming a major player had eluded their father. Since Miriam had taken the reins, his big sister had streamlined production, lowered costs and developed a nice, healthy bottom line.

Looked like Miriam thought the time to revisit the dream was now.

Apparently she planned to drag him along, too.

"And you want me to do the writing? Isn't that backwards? Aren't authors supposed to bring the completed manuscript to us?"

His sister straightened in the large executive leather chair. It had been their father's. That and the two leather seats in front of the desk were the only things she'd kept. The rest of the office had her stamp: rounded corners, sunburst motif—art deco all the way. "She's an academic, a doctor of anthropology as a matter of fact. Her writing is somehow, well, awkward."

How like his sister. She was tough as nails, battled reporters, distributors and every yahoo who didn't think she could run a company with the big boys. She was all business. But when it came to talent, she never liked to criticize anyone.

Years ago, Ian had found his sister's weak spot; she feared an utter lack of talent in herself. Artistically speaking. And to be honest, her fears were quite well-founded. She couldn't sing, dance, paint and her writing was terrible. Even her carefully worded memos to staff needed a good editor. So unlike their graceful and talented mother. So unlike him, minus the graceful.

Well, he liked to think he exuded grace in one area. In bed. No complaints there.

His sister called the doc's writing awkward. That must mean it read like an academic snooze fest.

"Why me?" he asked.

Miriam didn't meet his gaze. "Because you're my best reporter and photographer."

Ian dropped his elbows to his knees and leaned forward. "*Reporter* being the operative word there. Why would you want me to help write it?"

"You can work magic with words. And this project definitely needs some sparkle."

"Don't say *sparkle* around any of the guys. So what's the story about?"

"I haven't settled on a title yet, but she's calling it *Recipe for Sex.*" Miriam's brown gaze dropped from his.

Ian snorted. "Just to ensure I'll never be taken seriously in the world of journalism again?"

His sister shook her head, her dark hair not budging from the neat knot on top of her head. "You're a crime and war reporter. You're jaded. It's time to do a little something different."

Yes, and here it came. The big lecture on his lifestyle. He'd walk if she called him a danger junkie. But his sister was a businesswoman, and he knew how to fight dirty. He'd attack her bottom line.

He settled back against the leather chair. "Jaded appears to be selling. Readership's up twenty-five percent."

"And my migraines are up forty-five percent. One hundred percent because of you."

She couldn't be serious about yanking him. Hot stuff was brewing in South America. He itched to cover it. "What is it you're saying?"

"I'm saying you've become a pain in the ass. After your last series of escapades, I need to keep an eye on you."

Ian gritted his teeth. "You may be my big sister, but I'm plenty capable of taking care of myself."

"How about three arrests in two years in countries that change names as quickly as the next coup can be organized? How about the broken ribs you got while fighting some rebel over the film you shot? How about the—"

He cut her off before she really got into this topic. His dangerous lifestyle tended to prove a favorite of hers. "Those are occupational hazards."

Miriam smiled, her eyes taking on a serious gleam. Crap. Now he was in for it. A smile was never good from his sister. He'd seen too many smiles induce too many lawyers, investment bankers and arrogant reporters into a false sense of security. She *would* get what she wanted.

But then, as her beloved brother, he was usually immune.

"This book is important to the company. It's important to me. I want this transition to go smoothly, and I know you can deliver it."

His immunity held firm. "Not gonna happen."

"I promised Mom."

Well, hell. And yes, the smile still worked. He'd been sucker punched, and it was a low blow. Miriam was the only one who kept in semiregular contact with the woman who'd left when Ian had been a toddler.

Theirs was a relationship filled with uncomfortable telephone calls, stilted conversations and now an extra drink at dinner to make it all not seem so bad.

Ian didn't need that lone semester's worth of psychology to realize all three of them held some strange, undeniable need to gain the distant, nonmaternal woman's approval. The fact that his mother showed even a bit of concern was infuriating.

And gratifying.

"Think of it as a favor," his sister suggested.

He raised an eyebrow.

"A mandatory favor."

MIRIAM COLE WAS NOT a wimp. Although she certainly saw the advantages of acting like one now. Sending her brother to Oklahoma so she could practice her new-found faith in avoidance was really a new low for her.

Oh, well, it would be good for him.

But still…she'd never evaded anything in her life. And if anyone actually commented that the wadded-up pink While You Were Out slip shoved in the back of her desk drawer was a wee bit out of character for her usual tidy self, she'd add denial to her growing list of bad habits she didn't plan to shed.

She should run that message slip through her shredder. It had already been a week since Rich had placed it on the middle of her desk. Why was she still holding on to it? She had no intention of returning the call of good ol' five-times-in-one-night Jeremy. Or was it six?

She suppressed a shiver and smoothed her hair, even though she'd twisted her dark hair into a tight not-a-chance-of-escaping knot. Anything not to remind her of how Jeremy's fingers had sifted through the strands.

Okay six. It had been six times.

Miriam slumped in her chair and gave herself permission to wallow in her mistake. She was due. Why should her torment only be reserved for nighttime when she was alone in her apartment? Why not let Jeremy and his six times invade the one place she'd always been able to control?

She'd never given much thought to Oklahoma as a state. Nothing much more than football, cows and musicals about dancing cowboys. She hadn't been prepared for Jeremy.

The place had brought her down. One moment she

was driving and singing badly with a song on the radio. The next she was on the side of the road kicking her foot in frustration at the red dirt aligning the highway.

She'd have the magazine do an exposé on the hazards of scenic drives. They should be synonymous with stranded and not seeing another person for miles. The unsuspecting public ought to know.

One thing was for certain…she never planned to go there again. She could only hope her brother would fare better.

2

"ANYONE EVER TELL you that you have too much sex stuff?" Thad asked.

Ava Simms looked up to see her brother unpack a wooden replica of Monolob, the penis god from an ancient Slavic tribe.

"Careful with that," she told him. "It took me weeks to find someone who could craft that out of the native wood. I'd hate for anything to break off."

"By anything, I'm assuming you mean this ginormous penis."

Thad examined the lean figure with the gigantic proportions. Male proportions. There was only one protruding object that could break off. Disgusted, he set the figure on the shelf, then turned it so the statue's large appendage faced the wall. "It's hard enough to get a date without the womenfolk being exposed and comparing others to this."

Ava paused as she broke down another shipping box. "Since when do you have a problem getting a date? Usually there's a cadre of broken hearts left in your wake."

"I'm doing this for other men. We've got to stick to-gether when battling forces like these." Thad flexed his bicep in a symbol of unity.

Rolling her eyes, Ava tossed the now-flattened box in the pile of cardboard ready to go to the recycler. "For your information, the men of the tribe carved those as they reached puberty. Some would even string smaller replicas around their necks."

Thad laughed, and looked pointedly at the backside of the figurine. "You'll need to do a bit more research on this one, little sister. I can't imagine *any* man, from any century, parading penises around. Certainly not around his neck."

"Ah, yes, sometimes I forget about the male rules of the early twenty-first century. You know, there's a whole anthropological study there in itself. 'No talking in the bathroom,' 'eyes straight ahead at the urinal,' 'never ac-knowledge another man's penis.' Honestly, it's like ignoring the elephant in the room. Hey—"

Groaning, her brother raised a hand. "Don't even think about asking me to take you back to the men's room at the airport. It was a mistake. You and your scientific study."

"There might be valuable lessons there. Think about what a trained, yet unbiased eye could glean. Maybe true insight into the differences between the sexes."

"Yes, the differences are very obvious at a urinal. You could call it the Stall Theory. Sorry, Sis, but I doubt any serious academic publication would pick it up."

Ava sighed and returned her attention to the boxes. "Well, that would be no change from what's going on now. No peer-reviewed journals want to publish my research on the lost sexual customs of the world, either."

Thad stooped to pick up another box. "So that's why you decided to write it up as a book."

"That, and the fact my research funding dried up, and it's too late now to find a teaching job. No university would take me on until fall. And now the publisher wants to help me fine-tune it, make it more attuned to today's reader. Whatever that means. As if people won't find the way I've written on socio-cultural and kinship patterns attention grabbing."

"Yeah, I can see how that wouldn't be a problem," he told her drily.

Ava glanced over to see her brother's lips twisting into a smile. "Okay, maybe I could do with a little lightening up."

"Face it, Sis, you haven't been living in the real world for…well, at all. Mom and Dad toted you around to every dig since you could carry a shovel. Then you went straight to college and basically never left."

"You had those same experiences," she pointed out.

"Except I chose to have a life between classes." Thad placed his hands on her shoulders and she looked into the green eyes so much like her own. "You know what, I think not finding a job is a good thing for you."

Ava scoffed, her bangs ruffling. "Apart from the tiny problem of paying for food and utilities."

Thad wrapped his arm around her shoulders, drawing her beside his tall frame. Why did he have to inherit all the height genes?

They'd always been close. Sometimes they were the only two children on a dig site, and they'd grown to read each other's moods. "Ava, listen. This is your opportunity to fly. Mom and Dad didn't give you that name for you to sit and mope. Avis, our eagle, now's your time to soar. So you're not teaching anthropology to a bunch of freshmen who probably don't want to sit in your class anyway. That's a good thing."

"I just thought I'd always teach and lecture. Share the love of traditions and learning of other cultures to fresh, new young minds."

Another huge disappointment in the daughter department. She'd chosen to go for anthropology rather than follow her parent's path and continue their research in mythology and the ancient Greek cultures. They'd have loved nothing better than to always have her by their side at the digs in Greece—the magical place where her parents fell in love.

She had no doubt if she'd pursued archeology she would have found half a dozen jobs at any major university across the country. Her last name alone would guarantee it.

But she didn't want to rely on that last name even on such short notice.

So she didn't have a job. She didn't have anything published impressive enough to get her a job in her chosen field.

So what? She did have a prospect. In two days, Miriam Cole from Cole Publishing would be here to "help" her explore the concepts best suited for her book.

Writing her book with a little bit of help wasn't exactly how she'd planned to earn a paycheck…but she'd adapt. Wasn't that one of the cornerstones of her teaching anyway? How cultures, people, throughout time changed to meet the problems that faced them?

She could be flexible. She'd show Miriam just how interesting ancient dead cultures and their sexual habits could be. Show her that they were relevant to the twenty-first century woman.

"That's it," she said, suddenly ready to clear the moving distraction out of her way. She had a stage to set for the head of Cole Publishing.

"What's it?" Thad asked.

Determination filled her, and Ava squared her shoulders. "I'm going to demonstrate that this book can be exciting. That people will want to read it. I'm going to knock her socks off. When Miriam Cole gets here, I'll greet her in the ceremonial wedding attire of the Wayterian people."

Thad lost his smile. "Isn't that basically just pa—"

Ava smiled. "Exactly."

IAN CIRCLED AROUND THE one-way streets of downtown Oklahoma City for a third time, looking for a place to park. Why couldn't the doc live in a normal place, not some converted old warehouse? Like maybe some place that didn't need to be validated.

For that matter, why'd she have to live in flyover country anyway? At least he'd had no layovers. He estimated he'd lost two years of quality life just sitting in a plane due to a lack of direct flights. The skills paid off this time. With no connections, he had some uninterrupted hours to review the project.

Just as on any assignment, he liked the broad details, but kept away from the finer points so he wouldn't be biased in one direction over another. He'd spent the flight to Oklahoma reviewing the doc's work that she'd turned in to Miriam. The writing style was abysmal. Something between technical anthropological jargon and absolute incoherence.

The sex stuff was the only thing that seemed remotely promising. But discussing it with a grandma-like Margaret Mead stretched before him and seemed as tantalizing as many hours of cuddling and spooning.

Finally, he parked in the red brick garage he'd found, paid his five bucks and hiked the few blocks to her warehouse loft apartment, lugging his camera, minirecorder and laptop. He looked down at the paper in his hand confirming her address. Top floor. Of course. She buzzed him in, and he headed for the elevator. He hated elevators. Every family member he had insisted on living on the top floor. He'd rather be chased to the border than be trapped in a metal box suspended by a string.

This kind of elevator was awful, one of those large service lifts. He'd have to pull the top and bottom gate closed. He'd take the stairs. He'd hiked through worse, and with all his equipment strapped to his back.

There was no mistaking which apartment was the doc's. A brown ceramic snake stood beside the front door. A snake with large breasts and fake red flowers coming out of its mouth. Weird.

This photo shoot and discussion was going to be worse than he'd first imagined. His sister owed him something good after this. She'd have to send him someplace dirty. Somewhere he could trudge through swamps and fight off rebels as he followed a band of radicals, a camera in one hand, a knife in the other. Ah, good times.

He knocked on the door. A strange exotic scent lingered in the air, tantalizing his nose. Subtle, yet almost…arousing. He took a few more sniffs of the air, then realized the scent came from underneath the door. At least the doc would smell better than the radicals.

Impatient, Cole knocked again. He already hated the assignment. And the doc. Now she wasn't even here to greet him. He'd make his sister cook for that. She hated cooking. He was about to leave when he heard a noise behind the door. Then some strange, elemental music. Was that drums?

The knob twisted and the door opened.

"Welcome," said the woman in front of him, a smile forming along the red fullness of her lips.

"Pay—" he managed to get out then stopped.

He'd had a thought. It was there just a second ago.

The woman took a quick step backwards, the smile fading from her face. "I thought you were someone else."

"Paint."

Her eyes lowered, following the elaborate swirls and colors that adorned her skin. Paint and nothing much else. He tried to swallow. He'd obviously prejudged this assignment too harshly.

Her eyes met his squarely. Not a trace of embarrassment or awkwardness in her body language. "Yes, the Wayterian people would adorn themselves in paints before their wedding, signifying their past. After the ceremony they rinse off in each other's presence, starting clean and fresh together."

Her expression became neutral, and the light he'd spotted in her green eyes as she talked faded.

"But you're probably not interested in that. As I said, I thought you were someone else."

He made out a few words. *Paint. Rinse. Together.* This woman had an amazing husky voice to go along with her amazingly painted body.

She made to close the door.

Whoa. Time to get with the program. He stuck his foot out to block it. "Wait. You've been waiting for me. You're Dr. Simms. Right?"

The door opened a fraction wider, and the doc poked her head out. "Who wants to know?" she asked, her expression growing guarded. Maybe she should have thought about looking through her peephole before opening the door nearly naked. Maybe he should volunteer to give her a few instructions on personal safety.

"I'm Ian Cole. Of Cole Publishing." He held up his tripod. "See? Totally legit."

"I thought Miriam would be coming. Is she with you?" She stood on her tiptoes to see behind him. Lots of luck, she only came to his chin.

"I'm her brother."

The woman in front of him nodded, a hint of rec-ognition now in her green eyes. "Ah, yes. You do the reports from the war zones. Gripping photos. I did some research on Cole Publishing." The smile returned to the doc's face, and she opened the door. "I thought this painting ritual might be something good for the book."

With the door open, the full impact of the doc's body crashed into him once more. Paint and a loincloth. That was basically the composition of the outfit.

Cole wasn't a man who was easily surprised. But Ava Simms stunned the hell out of him.

Vibrant colors of blue, green and black in fancy swirls, circles and lines touched every inch of her body. Her breasts stood bare, although entirely covered in paint.

He'd seen his share of naked breasts in his time. Ex-cellent ones. In all shapes and sizes. Large breasts that spilled out of his hands. Small, high breasts that begged to be kissed. But his favorite had to be the ones before him, covered in paint, fully exposed, yet completely covered. Totally erotic.

She seemed to be waiting for something. With an effort he'd brag about later, he dragged his eyes slowly up her body once more.

"Would you like to join me?" she asked.

Hell, yeah.

And reveal his giant hard-on. No.

The doc turned, and Ian almost groaned. He'd always thought of himself as an ass man. And the doc's ass confirmed it. Firm, as though she'd performed quite a few of those dances she'd described in her manuscript.

Covered in some white piece of cloth that looked as if it had been ripped and tied around her waist. Paint from her body had smudged the cloth in a few places. He couldn't imagine the men of the Wayt—the Wabr— the Whateverian would stay in a shower, washing off paint, when they could be screwing. Had he ever seen such a beautiful pair of breasts?

Heaving the gear on his shoulders, he followed the doc inside her apartment. He'd send his sister a thank-you card later. Coles were always polite and followed proper etiquette. They learned it from the cradle.

Ava pointed to her coffee table, covered by tubs filled with paint. "I was thinking that in the book we could give demonstrations on how to paint your lover's body. That's not totally in the Wayterian tradition, but we could still include the shower."

He didn't spy any paintbrushes. Images of sliding paint on this woman's body with his fingers, of her running her paint-smeared palms against his skin, then warm water cascading down their naked bodies together left him speechless.

The doc turned and raised an eyebrow. "Do you think men would find the ritual interesting?"

Well, *interesting* was one word for it.

He'd expected boring and painful when he flew to this assignment. Boring was out. He adjusted his pants, but it was going to be painful. Definitely painful.

Dr. Ava Simms was nobody's grandma.

3

"So why did your sister send you? I thought she was coming herself."

A look of unease crossed Ian's face. Ava saw his lips move. Did he just mumble? It almost sounded like he muttered something about cowardly sisters.

"Mr. Cole?" she prompted.

"I'll be taking the photos for the book, and revising the manuscript." He hunched down to his equipment bag.

Bringing in a photographer was a given. The rituals she wanted to explore were also very visual. Men were very visual creatures and most cultures had adapted to that. Her book would have to include a lot of pictures to be appealing to her target males. "I thought this meeting with Miriam was to refine and make some fixes to my writing. Surely *revising* is too strong a word," she prodded.

He pulled out what looked to be a light meter. Her father often used the more sophisticated photographic equipment while on a dig site.

"Mr. Cole, are you listening to me?"

"Call me Ian."

She narrowed her gaze. This man was trying *not* to

tell her something. Something he didn't want her to know. She'd studied cultures from all over the world, and men from one continent to another flashed the same visual cues when wanting to avoid a direct question. Especially from a woman.

The shifting weight from foot to foot.

The suddenly moving hands.

The rapid eye movement.

Yes, Ian Cole was in full avoidance mode, exhibiting the number-one classic sign—sidestepping the question.

"Ian, when you say revising, what you really mean is—"

His gaze met hers finally. Clear, brown and full of truth. A truth he didn't want to tell her.

"Ghost-writing. Miriam feels the pages you sent in have too much of an academic feel to them," he said, cutting her off with a hint of apology in his voice.

At least he was honest. Disappointed, she slumped against a nearby column. The cool wood cut into the bare skin of her back, and she cringed.

Obviously she'd failed in her quest to find the creative "wow" to impress her new publisher. Maybe her *only* shot at a publisher. This was a disaster. No one wanted her work in the academic field. Now it seemed no one wanted her work outside of it, either.

Ava wanted to kick the wall in frustration. She hadn't realized until just this moment how important doing this book on her own had been to her.

"Have a seat," she told him with a sigh.

Quickly, he shifted his gear. With one direct look

into her eyes he sat down. Was that concern she spotted in his gaze?

Now that she knew what she was dealing with, she could move forward. Funny, she'd never acknowledged how correctly her mother had pegged her daughter's personality. Mom had always compared her to a triangle: didn't matter which way she pointed as long as she was moving in some direction.

She'd never had her own apartment before. The closest thing she'd had to a home had been her dorm room. She had no idea if she'd placed the couch or the end tables in the right places, but she liked the final result, and that was all that mattered. She watched Ian look around.

He finished his examination with a slow whistle between his teeth after looking up. "Wow, this is some place. That ceiling is amazing."

"It makes me feel like I'm not so boxed in. I like wide-open spaces."

"Yeah? Me, too." A smile tugged at his top lip, and his gaze narrowed.

For a moment, she met his eyes. Where had her instincts gone? She was supposed to be the expert. *She* should be the one to find common ground. *That* was how alliances were formed. And right now she sensed she needed Ian on her side to get what she wanted—to write this book on her own.

On to step two: Slowly layer in personal experiences so that it's harder for the target to say no. Her gaze slid upwards. "When I saw the high ceiling, I knew this had

to be my apartment. This used to be an old warehouse."
She pointed to the exposed ductwork, painted a warm
taupe. "The nearly floor-to-ceiling window allows in
great natural light, which just feels more normal to me,
even though I'm living six flights up."

"You spend a lot of time outdoors?"

Ava laughed softly. "Since I can remember. Not
many hotels in the isolated regions my parents took me
to. My father liked to sleep under the stars."

"This your first time living in a city?" he asked.

Questions. Of course, she should have realized. Ian
was a reporter. He'd be a man who'd ask a lot of questions. Was she slipping that fast now that she wasn't
active in the field?

Hmm. He was making her a subject. He'd apparently
acquired his own approach—to remain distant.

Questions were fine. She could handle questions.
Her mission was to make sure her answers steered him
away from viewing her as a writing project.

"Other than college towns, I don't think I've ever
lived someplace with over a thousand people. To go to
someplace with more than half a million people was a
pretty big leap. I thought about living in the rural area
of the state, then I figured, what the hell?"

His brown gaze met hers. Did she see a bit of under-
standing in the depths of his eyes? Clearly he was a man
who understood a what-the-hell? sentiment.

"I have a gorgeous view of Oklahoma City's skyline.
The city is literally my backyard. And I have plenty of
space to show off the artwork and sculptures I've col-

lected from some of the places I've visited. Before he left, my brother installed shelving on almost every available wall space." She loved the results.

Ian nodded, and ran his finger along the fine woodwork of the nearest bookcase. His hands were work-rough appealing. Obviously he didn't use a phone or computer to do his research, he was in the field. Just like her.

Ava smiled when she realized his attention had settled on a small collection of naked fertility goddesses.

"Ah, you've found my harem. As you can see, most fertility deities are shown with large breasts and protruding bellies."

Ian pointed to Danisis, a voluptuous-looking goddess. "She's different from the others."

"She's my favorite. She's the goddess of war and fertility. Kind of ironic, huh? One destroys life, the other creates it. I love the spear she's carrying, the detail work is amazing. There's a very erotic love-play ritual associated with her."

His hand lowered and he went back to his bags. "Where do you want me to stash my gear? I'll need to plug in my laptop. My battery's shot—I used it on the plane."

"We can just use my computer. My manuscript is already right there."

Ian shook his head. "It would work better to use my laptop. First, if we go from your manuscript, it'll be too tempting to use what's already there. We need to start fresh. A total rewrite."

She took a deep breath, steeling herself for her next question. She *had* to know. "It was that bad, huh?"

The left side of his mouth lifted. Was that almost a smile? "A woman who wants me to tell it like it is."

"Always," she replied. She wasn't one for sugar-coating, she wanted total honesty.

"It sucked. And not in a good way."

Ava gasped. Okay, maybe not that much honesty. "Is there a good way to suck?" she asked.

Ian coughed behind his hand, then looked at her strangely. "If you were going for campy humor, then bad writing can make it more fun. Sometimes. Probably never."

She nodded. A flash of alarm crossed Ian's face. His eyes widened, and for a moment Ava was confused.

"Your concept is excellent," he hastily reassured her. Awkwardly. What did he think she was going to do, cry? That explained the alarm she'd sensed in him a moment ago. Often in patriarchal societies, men backed away from tears. Anything squishy, like emotions, were very much off limits.

"Thanks," she told him firmly. But he didn't need to worry about her. This was science. There was no emotion in science.

"It's just the writing. The rituals and foods you chose were perfect examples of new and unusual, yet didn't morph into the freak zone."

Her eyes narrowed. That would be a relief for the cultures who'd shared their revered customs and ceremonies with her—that they hadn't moved into Mr. Cole's freak category.

Which then drew the question—what *was* Mr. Cole's freak category?

And would it mesh with her freak categories?

No, she didn't care. This man simply didn't get what she was trying to do here. She didn't want his help, plus he didn't have the sensitivity. Although she hadn't expected to spend any time with the man, his name had come up when she'd Googled Cole Publishing. Her search proved him to be a man more in tune covering the world's hot zones. How would a man like that possibly understand what she was trying to do here? He'd have to go.

"We'll go over each chapter. We can take the pictures as we move along or do them all at once at the end. At night in my hotel room, I'll edit."

"*You'll* edit?" she asked, her tone unbelieving.

Ian ticked off these items as if they were on a to-do list. He'd only reduced her life's work and passion into something resembling an inventory sheet. "You can simply crank these out?" she asked, wanting to make sure.

"I'll have this book whipped into shape in no time."

"*You'll* have it whipped into shape?" Yes, and there was her limit. Ian Cole had just stepped over the line. She squared her shoulders and looked him straight in the eye. Ian's gaze lowered a fraction before returning to hers.

She shook her head. "No. I can't possibly have you do the writing."

"Why?" he asked. His voice held no offense. And yet that one word sounded unbending. As if he fully expected to get his way.

"It's clear you don't appreciate what I'm trying to do with this book. You're thinking to spice up the time in the bedroom, not how the act of lovemaking can be enhanced with a few delicacies and rites from other cultures."

Ian moved toward her, towering above her. Something sparked inside those jaded eyes of his, and the firmness of his lips softened. Grew more sensual. For the first time, she felt crowded in her apartment.

"Oh, really?" he said.

She gulped. "Yes, really."

"This book is supposed to be about passion," he said, his voice soft, like warm honey. "Fire. The words and pictures should put a fire in your blood. Bring a woman and a man closer. Sharing the deep-rooted coming together of men and women from the beginning of time eternal. From all over the world. It should connect. It should be elemental. Raw. Man. Woman. Sex."

Ava swallowed. Her blood felt heated, and yet she shivered.

Okay. So maybe this man got it. Her heartbeat quickened with each word from his mouth. With every firm declaration he stated, a picture formed in her mind. A picture of bringing woman and man closer. Of bringing Ian closer to her. Elemental. Connecting and raw.

She took a deep breath. Bad move. He smelled good. Real good, like the rain forest after a heavy downpour. Earthy and clean.

Pheromones. That's all it was. Ian Cole exuded pheromones she just happened to respond to. It was science. It wasn't emotion. Now was the time for her to think logically. To be fair, he'd conveyed the concept better than she had, and it was her creation.

Now *that* made her mad.

"What you have is more along the lines of insert tab A into slot B with a lot of history thrown in to make sure you'd rather mow the lawn than spend hours making love to a sensual woman," he said. His words were laced with amusement.

Though to her they were like a splash of cold water to her heated skin.

Okay, she was not about to have her project be just another in a long line of screwups because of a little estrogen. Maybe Miriam's idea of bringing in Ian Cole would work. He might have something to add. But there'd have to be some ground rules, and *she'd* have to make the final decisions.

"Maybe we can try this," she hedged. Ava tapped her foot. What she needed was some brainstorming, paradigm shifting. She'd planned on this project being solely her creation, she'd not factored—

"Don't you want to cover yourself up?"

Ava shrugged, and looked down at her body. She'd been so used to walking around nearly naked from one setting to another, she'd almost forgotten she wore little else but paint and a loincloth. Most cultures didn't have a fully-clothed policy the way her homeland did. It wasn't uncommon to go topless.

Was Ian a prude?

His gaze never left her face.

Come to think of it, when she'd opened the door to him earlier, there had been a sudden leap of something in his eyes, something base and hot. His jaded exterior had quickly masked that.

Once or twice it had seemed his gaze drifted downward, but he quickly raised his eyes right back up to meet hers. Or he looked at her high ceiling. Or her statues.

This was something telling. Ian Cole wanted to avoid looking at her body. Now this was good to know.

Maybe he did share that erotic picture his words had conjured up in her mind.

IAN KNEW HE WAS in trouble the moment her eyes turned assessing. Damn it, he was usually much better at hiding his naked interest in a woman. But then, that was the problem. Ava stood before him basically naked. His body liked it. He liked it.

He watched as Ava glanced at her paint-covered body. Some of it erotically smudged right now. She tilted her head and he made eye contact with the brilliant green of her eyes.

Keep looking up, buddy.

"Why?" she asked, her voice not sounding confused or innocent. Just curious.

Why what? He forgot what they were talking about. And he had a sneaking suspicion he was the one who'd started this particular vein of conversation. "Uh…"

Trying to get her into bed while they worked on the

book was a bad idea. If he had to work without sleep to get this book written quickly, that would just have to be the price he paid. Hell, he'd go without food, too.

Had he just decided to sleep with Ava Simms? When had he decided that?

About two seconds after spotting her.

That was a bad idea. Really bad. He'd list the multitude of reasons right now. Except none really came to mind at the moment because a nearly naked, gorgeous woman stood before him. How was a man supposed to work in these conditions?

This woman must be covered as soon as possible. Cover. That was it. That's what he asked about. "Don't you want to put something on?"

She shrugged again. "Not really. And this way I can show you some of the pattern work."

It had been his experience that most women had at least one body part they felt self-conscious about. He wouldn't have complained if his former girlfriends had wanted to parade around in next to nothing. It's just that they hadn't. In fact, he'd seen them go to Herculean efforts to cover their thighs with a sheet, or hips with a towel.

It was all ridiculous. Women were beautiful. The key was to find that one part they hated, and then issue compliments. It never failed.

But this woman seemed to have no problem parading around in barely anything.

She lightly touched a rounded circle of blue on her arm. "You see, the woman begins by painting the color blue on her body. This represents the sky and water. Sky and water play a large role in the lore of many cultures around the world."

He nodded, his gaze shifting from her face to her arm. *Don't look to the right.* Although he already knew what he'd see. Her beautiful breasts painted yellow.

"Now did that bother you? That insertion of a little history?"

Not a bit. He shook his head as his mouth watered.

"That's the approach I think we should take." Ava trailed her fingers along the green lines crisscrossing on her thighs. "The green represents the earth. New and unknown. Ready to be explored."

He grew harder as she touched and stroked her skin. His fingers ached to do the same. To trace the green lines, to smudge the blue paint on her body.

"Yellow is the past. The Wayterian people don't place value on virginity, so a woman may have had several lovers. Do you?"

"Do I what?" he asked, suddenly feeling as if he'd been jerked out of a sex fantasy.

"Place value on virginity?"

"I'm not one if that's what you're asking."

A smile curved along her lips. "Good. I wouldn't want you cowering in the corner."

She was laughing at him.

Toying with him, in fact. He should be irritated. Instead he found himself turned on more. Well, two could play that game. He deliberately lowered his eyes to her yellow-painted breasts. "That's a very bright color."

"The Wayterian women coat the yellow paint on their breasts. Once the new husband and wife are alone, she takes his hands and places them on her breasts."

Her nipples hardened before his eyes. She might be toying with him to get a reaction, but she wasn't immune to him, either.

"The paint never completely dries, so some of the color gets on him, as well. Together they wash the paint, the past, away. They become one, joined by sky, water and earth."

Ian closed his eyes for a moment, imagining washing the paint off this woman's body. And Ava washing the color from his skin. Erotic and charged. It was perfect for the book.

"I think this ceremony is beautiful." Her voice lost its challenging playfulness of earlier. "I'm always moved by the meaning behind the acts."

And surprisingly, he was, too.

She swallowed, and took a step away from him. "Well, since you're familiar with this particular rite now, I'll just hop into the shower and remove the paint. I won't be long and then we can get started."

Ian raised his hand, not bothering to hide the look of disbelief he was sure was on his face. "Wait a minute. Are you about to go and take a shower leaving a man you've known about ten minutes alone in your apartment?"

For the first time since she'd opened the door, Ava looked unsure. She shifted her balance, and crossed her arms. "I, uh, guess that I was."

"Lady, you've been out in the wild too long. You can't be so trusting."

She shrugged her shoulders. "You're Miriam's brother. It's not like she'd send a serial killer. It will only take me a few minutes."

He couldn't picture sitting calmly on her couch waiting while she showered. Imagining her naked. And wet. He almost groaned.

No. Not going to happen. He had to get out of there. "I'll check in to the hotel while you're getting ready. I'm going to grab a bite to eat. The sandwich on the plane could pass for a hockey puck."

"Oh, I'm getting hungry, too. Why don't we meet at one of the restaurants down on the canal for a late lunch? You up for Mexican?"

He was up for anything about now. "Sounds good." Ava turned on her heel, and once again he got a view of her great ass. "I'll pick you up from here."

She stopped and glanced at him over her shoulder. "Is this about the shower thing? Don't worry, I don't need an escort to keep me safe. Besides, you looked pretty trustworthy to me."

Trustworthy. *Trustworthy?* No one had ever accused him of being trustworthy before. Like a teddy bear. Or a cute puppy. That was almost insulting. Ian straightened his shoulders. He was dangerous. A man of the world. Wanted by the law in three countries. At least. He was *not* a teddy bear.

He'd put an end to that. "Let me know if you need some help with the second part of the ritual," he said.

"The second part?" she asked.

"The washing off."

Her full bottom lip curled upward, and a naughty twinkle appeared in her eyes. "I'll let you know," she told him.

Now why did that come out sounding like a promise?

4

WHILE THE WATER for the shower heated, Ava quickly typed in the Web site for Cole Publishing. She punched his name in the search fields.

"Bingo." Over thirty results popped up on her screen. She selected the one at the top, and her screen immediately filled with his image. Obviously the picture on his bio page must have been taken a few years ago. In the photo, he had a friendly smile and the look of someone ready to tackle the world.

Much how she'd felt five seconds before she opened the door to him.

Now Ian wore that world-weary air. The stress lines around his mouth were deeper now than the laugh lines around his eyes. She'd seen his type in the airport. They huddled around their gates, ready to hit the next political hot spot.

She headed anyplace but there.

A puff of steam enticed her into the bathroom. Tugging off her loincloth, Ava stepped beneath the spray.

The warm water glided around her body, smearing the paint further. The yellows and blues fused together, turning green and pooling at her feet before sliding down the drain. Long, hot showers. Steam and heat and the scent of honeysuckle. Now this was something she had missed.

Ava reached for the soap and bubbled up a rich lather. Although the paint was easy to smear, it wasn't the easiest to remove from her skin.

Of course Ian had offered to help. She smiled again, thinking how his brown eyes had turned darker when he'd made the invitation. Ava had seen the desire in his direct gaze. He hadn't tried to mask it. She liked that about him.

A direct man voiced exactly what he wanted. Sought to fulfill his woman's desires. She would have hated to take suggestions on her book from a man who couldn't handle the naturalness of sex. Afraid of his own desires.

And of hers.

There'd been sex in his eyes. Sex on his mind. Despite the warmth of the water, her nipples hardened as she remembered that brown-eyed gaze of his sliding down her body.

When had sex come into play? She wondered as she reached for a bright yellow sponge. When did sex *not* come into play between a man and a woman? Despite Ian's obvious assumption that she was a bit on the naive side, she'd studied gender differences enough to know that one thing shared by both men and women was a charged curiosity whenever they were in each other's presence. A curiosity about nakedness. Would he groan? Would she scream?

It all happened within the first five seconds of meeting someone new, the mind and body put that person into three categories. Yes, no and maybe.

And right now her body was thinking yes. What would sex with Ian be like? Sex had been in Ian's eyes, which placed Ava in his hell-yes category.

If they were going to collaborate, attraction between them probably wasn't the best situation. Far off the mark from professionalism. But then, who was she to shy away from sexual attraction?

Come to think of it, sexual tension and desire between the two of them might be a good thing. Heat might translate onto the pages, into their very writing. Craving the carnal would implicitly lace their words with an intense hunger for sex.

A shiver raced down her spine. Now *this* was something that would sell. She should go for it. Why not suffer for her art?

Anxious to get to work, she sudsed her arms and legs, the water and bubbles turning her already sensitive skin into taut nerves waiting to be touched. Caressed. Her skin tingled.

She reached for the soft washcloth, and twisted out the excess water. Ava stroked the cloth against her breasts, wiping away the more stubborn yellow paint. As she rubbed the cloth against her nipple, the skin along her neck and her breasts turned bumpy and sensitive. Tingles from her nipples shot downward.

She washed her other breast, then slowly trailed the cloth down along her ribcage, around her navel. The material felt rougher now against the heightened sensitivity of her flesh. She imagined Ian's work-roughened hands on her. Imagined him caressing her the same way as the washcloth.

A bit of the cloth tickled the skin of her inner thigh and she sucked in a breath. Steam surrounded her, a light caress against her body. The humid air inside the shower filled her lungs and she leaned against the tile wall for support.

The water ran between her legs, and she followed the trail with the washcloth. She clamped her eyes shut when the cloth grazed her clitoris. Delicious sensations quivered along every nerve. She stroked herself and moaned.

Some ancients believed a couple learned to please their mate only after watching them pleasure themselves. She imagined Ian outside her shower door, watching her touch herself. Becoming aroused.

Then she imagined him joining her in the shower, imagined herself watching him take his cock in his hand. Seeing it grow harder and bigger as he stroked himself, showing her how he liked to be touched. How he wanted her to touch him.

She pressed against her clit, her body growing tense. She gasped and her muscles tightened.

No.

If she brought her own release now, some of the tension and heat that zinged between them wouldn't be as strong. She wanted her pleasure to be on the edge, near the top. Not satiated.

An old woman she'd met in Australia once had told her the greatest aphrodisiac for a man was a woman's arousal.

Maybe now she would put that woman's theory to the test. Might make an interesting chapter for the book. Goose bumps rose on her skin as the spray massaged every muscle. She'd definitely suffer for that chapter.

With her body still humming, she quickly finished her shower.

IT DIDN'T TAKE IAN long to check in to the Bricktown Hotel; a chain hotel that catered to businesspeople, where the staff was usually friendly and efficient. Since his laptop battery was dead, he plugged the computer in first thing. This hotel promised to be the "most wired hotel in Oklahoma City." Most hotel claims were wrong, but he needed this one to be right.

He was used to traveling light. He'd packed for a week, but figured that would be more than enough time to get this book on track.

If Ava Simms didn't kill him. Some women shouldn't be allowed out of the house. She definitely needed a warning label. Loss of blood to the brain.

Crossing to the sink, he turned on the taps. He splashed water onto his face, washing away the travel grime. Ava would be in the shower now. Naked and wet. No matter how good-looking a woman was, she always looked just a little bit better wet.

He imagined Ava wet and nude under the spray of the shower.

With a groan, he wiped his face with a towel. Glancing at his watch he saw he still had about fifteen minutes to kill. His cell phone rang, and he pulled it from his waist to check at the caller ID. His sister. Good. He was in a mood to harass her over this assignment.

"Did you meet the doc?" she asked.

"Two days. I'm giving this two days, then I'm out of hell."

"I have every faith in you."

OVER THE YEARS, HER brother had been shoved into filthy, rat-infested prisons, slopped around in some of the world's most disease-ridden swamps and suffered weather hardships and clean-water deprivation of the likes she could only imagine. All to get the story.

And yet *this* assignment was the one he compared to hell. She almost laughed.

Miriam fingered the glass paperweight on her desk. She should feel guilty about sending her brother someplace she knew he'd hate. She should, but she was in full self-preservation mode.

Her brother's vehemence had been surprising. She'd dwell on it if another pink message slip hadn't appeared under the paperweight. Miriam wadded the paper up into a tight ball and aimed it toward her trash can. She missed by a good six inches.

Her aim was going the same way as her judgment. She was making a poor business decision and that wasn't like her. Things *would* have been smoother if she'd gone to Oklahoma with Ian. That was her element. What she did. Some people could cook. Some could write. *She* could multitask.

Miriam was a whiz at juggling millions of details, all

while keeping overblown egos and hurt feelings to a minimum. Nothing was ever personal and people left her office with a smile even if they came away with less than their asking price.

A few days with the doc and her brother and this book would be complete and ready to go into production and she'd be making more money for the company. So why not?

Jeremy.

If she went back to Oklahoma, she would surely contact him.

On the one hand, that wouldn't be such a bad thing. Who couldn't handle six or seven times a night?

Her nipples hardened and her skin tingled under her clothes. What was she mulling over a moment ago? The book she'd risked her reputation and quite a bit of money on. That book.

This was why six or seven times a night would be bad. She'd get nothing done. Her skin grew hot. She felt uncomfortable. *No.* Not uncomfortable…irritated. She'd think of it as irritated and chafed. In fact, that's exactly what she should be doing. Word association when thoughts of Jeremy popped into her mind. All of them bad.

Those gorgeous blue eyes of his. Same color as the first car that ever side-swiped her.

Those long showers together. Dry skin.

Seven or eight times a night? Bladder infection.

Miriam slumped in her chair and scanned her office walls. Here was her family history, the legacy she was now in charge of safeguarding. Rows of framed magazine covers lined each wall. Some black and white, others in bold color. Through war, the baby boom, flower power, disco to iPod, Coles had guided the company sensibly and competently.

And not a single Cole had ever blown it over a romance. Although her dad had come close when he'd married her mom. Miriam had always thought herself more like her grandfather. Now it was clear she'd inherited her father's self-destructive romantic habits. Obviously embraced them because she couldn't get that man out of her mind.

Her glance hit upon one of the covers. Woman in a business suit, power bun with the buttons on her silk blouse undone to reveal a sexy red bra.

Is All Work and No Play Making Jane a Dull Girl?

She reread the caption once more. Her shoulders relaxed and a smile slowly started to spread across her lips. It was strange how often something on one of these covers would trigger an emotion or a decision.

Yes. She had become a very dull girl. Miriam had been nothing but work for a very long time. When was the last time she'd gone out? How many times had she turned down her friends' invitations to hit the town? When was the last time *she'd* been inclined to wear a sexy red bra?

What was wrong with her? She lived in the town that never slept. And she'd been in most nights by nine. She needed to get out. Meet new and interesting men. Laugh, dance. Of course, seven or eight times seemed great when you hadn't gotten any in seven or eight months.

This had nothing to do with Jeremy at all. She picked up her cell phone to call Jenna. That speed-dial setting hadn't been used in ages.

Except Rich buzzed in over the intercom.

"Ms. Cole, there's someone here to see you."

She scanned the schedule Rich placed on her desk every morning. She didn't have any appointments. Rich would know not to announce a drop-in. Something was odd.

"It's a Mr. Kelso."

Miriam could tell by Rich's tone that this name was supposed to mean something to her. It didn't.

"A Mr. *Jeremy* Kelso."

Miriam clicked her phone closed.

5

IAN GRIMACED. He studied his hotel room. Already he had done all he needed to do. And still he felt restless.

So what else was new? Seems he'd battled restlessness for as long as he remembered. Why stay in the same place when something else beckoned around the corner? Hell on relationships.

But then, he wasn't much of a relationship kind of guy.

So then why did the doc get to him?

She was just another woman. Same as any woman from any other part of the world. Granted her parts were naked and covered with paint…but still.

Ian paced toward his window. He needed outside. He needed the sun on his head and a breeze against his face. Sixth-story windows in hotels did not cut it. He pushed himself away from the glass. He'd walk back to Ava's apartment, and skip all elevators. That should burn off some energy.

Like Ava's place, the hotel faced the winding canal of downtown Oklahoma City, and so the walk to meet her wouldn't take long.

He hiked down the stairs and emerged into the sunlight, giving in to the restlessness. The canal waters rippled bluish-green a few feet away from him. Trees and flowers flanked the stonework path beside the water. He weaved among the mothers pushing strollers who seemed to be the predominant occupants of the walk during the middle of the day.

Old warehouses being turned into stunning homes had renewed many an old downtown area suffering from urban blight. Oklahoma City obviously reaped the same benefits. Restaurants bracketed the walk, so he suspected couples would be replacing the moms and joggers once the dinner hour arrived.

A bright-yellow boat floated below him, passengers waving to the pedestrians. They waved back. His lips twisted. Flyover country. People didn't wave to one another in the places he'd been.

He found Ava waiting for him outside the entrance to her building.

A blonde.

Ava was a blonde. He hadn't been able to tell earlier. All the paint was gone, and her hair was still damp from her shower. Natural highlights from the sun streaked her hair. He'd never gone for blondes before, preferring the dark and exotic over the coolness of many fair-haired women. And those green eyes of hers were anything but cool.

He felt anything but cool around Ava. She smiled and came toward him, and his eyes were immediately drawn to her body. His normal life felt a world away from the utter temptation that was this woman. His days and nights were filled with the exciting challenges of chasing down people who did not want to be found, rough terrain and hanging out with guys who smelled like something rotten.

So on the blessed, and lately, more rare occasions when he was with a woman, he wanted soft curves, sweet scents and her dressed in pure glamour. When they weren't naked, that is.

None of that remotely described Ava. Oh, he liked her curves, but there was nothing sweet about this woman. And nothing wrong with the casual jeans and animal-print top she wore.

She hadn't bothered to put on any makeup, and he liked her natural like this. A light layer of freckles dusted her nose and cheeks. Like him, Ava was apparently a woman who'd spent some time in the sun.

She also smelled like cinnamon.

And he loved the smell of cinnamon.

"I found the Mexican place on my way over here. You ready?" he asked her. Ready to get back on the move. Bad things always happened when you stayed in one place.

Ava nodded. "At night they cook their tortilla chips, and I can smell it for hours in my apartment. Sometimes I wake up craving Mexican food, and I didn't even do that when I lived there."

"Then what are we waiting for? Let's go." He adjusted his larger steps to hers. Her head just reached his shoulders. The scent of cinnamon surrounded him once more.

"How'd you wind up in Oklahoma?" he asked, digging up a way to get his mind off the smell of her hair. He was a reporter. He asked questions.

"My grandparents live here. In fact, that was their building. I wouldn't have been able to afford this many square feet. My parents were always moving us from one place to another, but we'd always spend our holidays in Oklahoma. It seemed natural to set up a home base here when I returned from overseas."

"Was that often?" he asked. Talk. Talk was good. It took his mind off wondering what she wore under her shirt. Wondering whether she preferred animal print in all the clothes that touched her skin...

Hell, it'd been a while since he'd been with a woman, but usually he could go longer than ten seconds before imagining her naked.

"From my earliest memories. The longest I can remember staying anywhere was two years. It feels kind of weird to be opening boxes instead of packing them. Some of these things I haven't seen in years."

Her apartment had been filled with statues, masks and pictures. It didn't feel like a home base to him. A home base was more like his apartment, a place to sleep and watch football until the next assignment put you in harm's way. There was nothing permanent about a home base, and Ava's apartment felt very permanent.

"Were your parents anthropologists like you?" He did not need to know this. Knowing her background wasn't important for the writing of this book. He'd only meant to talk, to pass the time, to distract himself. But he found himself curious about her answers. He'd met a lot of different people during his travels. Why did he care?

A smile touched her lips, and she laughed softly. He liked the sound of her laugh. "I'm not laughing at you. It's just that it isn't very often people don't know who my parents are, but then, I'm mainly hanging out with a bunch of academics. My parents, Carol and Alex Simms, uncovered a temple to Isis in ancient Greece and set the archeology world on its ear."

"Oh, really? And how would one do that exactly?" During his flight to meet Ava, he couldn't have imagined anything more boring than having a conversation about archeology. Now he was intrigued.

"One would do that by saying that that temple proved the ancient Greeks patterned their gods and goddesses on those of the Egyptians, in the same way that the Romans took over the Greek gods and goddesses. It's not even too far a stretch to get from Horus to Zeus."

He whistled. "Wow, pretty radical."

"And pretty controversial."

"So why anthropology?" There was the curiosity again. He didn't need to know anything personal about her to make this book work.

"It wasn't too far a stretch. Apparently, wanting to uncover something is in the genes I inherited from them. But on the digs, I was always more interested in the people who'd evolved from the particular culture my parents were studying. How many of the same practices they kept, and which they didn't. That kind of thing."

They rounded another corner and found themselves standing in front of the Mexican restaurant. A hostess quickly took them to a balcony table overlooking the canal water.

Ian cut a glance in her direction as she silently perused her menu. His reporter instincts reappeared. There was something interesting here about the doc. Ava had a degree most people only used for teaching. Also, she wasn't out in the field—another possibility with her degree. And she hadn't followed in the family tradition.

Forget about her. Write the book, then move on.

"What do your parents think of you writing this book?" he found himself asking. *Subtle, you jerk.*

She lifted an eyebrow. "The sex research? Well, as they, too, were researchers, sex was pretty much part of the dinnertime conversation with my parents."

Sex *never* figured into his family's dinnertime conversation.

"Just look around a Roman coliseum or inside a pyramid, and you'll see sex everywhere. Both Mom and Dad were very matter-of-fact about it."

That explained a lot. Ava could talk about sex the way some way people talked about their laundry. And yet, her voice took a husky dip when she said the word *sex*. Maybe prancing around nearly naked in front of him had affected her, as well. Now *this* was starting to go somewhere.

"You're not answering the question. Do they like what you're doing?"

Her eyes met his, and she pushed a strand of her drying blond hair behind her ear. "They hate it. They think I'll never be taken seriously in the academic field."

"You're writing a book."

"A pop-fiction book. That's like intellectual prostitution in their opinion. Oh, don't get me wrong, they're not snobs, they're just…"

"Academics?" he suggested.

Ava nodded, and that lock of hair fell forward again from behind her ear. He itched to touch the strands. To let them fall through his fingers. "They don't think anyone will ever take my research seriously after this."

"Will they?" he asked, and wondered why he'd be concerned about that. Cole Publishing was in the business of making money, and although he wasn't sure about it on the plane, he knew they could make a lot with this book…with the proper execution.

"Probably not," she said, her tone rueful. "But then, no one has really taken my work seriously. More like facts to parade out at Valentine's Day. Colleges prefer professors who get published in professional journals, and bring in grant money. Groundbreaking—not titillation."

If they didn't take her seriously before, they certainly wouldn't now. Maybe he should give her one last warning. He'd hate for her to regret writing the book. The enthusiasm had faded from her voice, and a line formed on her forehead.

Then her face brightened and she stunned him with a beautiful smile. His pulse quickened. "Screw 'em. That's why I'm doing the book."

"Beat them at their own game." He liked that about her. He was beginning to like a lot of things about her.

"So why call the book *Recipe for Sex?* That title is all wrong, by the way. I'll brainstorm a list tonight, and give you a heads-up in the morning."

"Why don't I brainstorm a list and give you the heads-up in the morning?"

His lips twisted for a moment, then he grinned. "Going to be like this, is it? Fight me every step of the way?"

"As the writer, I should make the final decisions."

He raised an eyebrow. "I was brought in to fix some of those decisions."

"And I'll take your suggestions under advisement," she told him.

Ian laughed. "Glad to hear it," he said in the tone of a man confident he'd get his way. "The title still won't work. It sounds like a cookbook."

"Well, originally I thought I'd just include the foods that put couples, and particularly men, in the mood."

"Why men?" he asked.

"It's been my experience, and I can document this with culture after culture, that men don't often use food in their seduction."

Now wait a minute, he made a mean lasagna. He'd be happy to make it for her. And if they managed to get a little messy and needed to clean up together...so be it.

"I can see by your face you don't agree. In cultures where couples routinely push back marriage and family, then yes, the male will cook. In fact, most men have one 'signature' dish they believe is the ultimate key to the hookup."

Ian cleared his throat. Okay, he made other things besides lasagna. "That's ridiculous."

She smiled then nodded. "Research only gives us generalities. Individuals can always surprise you. One thing that is a fact is a man's sense of smell. It's very powerful. A potent scent can stimulate blood flow to the extremities, including the penis, and can evoke all sorts of feelings."

"In the book, we'll use another word other than *feelings* for the male readers."

"You know, straying from gentler emotions isn't universal among men."

"It will be for the men we're trying to sell this book to." And if he had to hear the word *penis* from her lips again, he'd have to resort to phoning this book in.

Change the subject. "Let's get back to this smell thing. Why is it women are always wanting to smell flowers? I could care less."

"Because that's the wrong smell for a man. Believe it or not, the scents more attractive to men are food-related. There's something to be said for that old saying about the way to a man's heart is through his stomach. Pumpkin, for instance, elicits very strong responses from men. And the smell of doughnuts."

"We can keep a running list of places for women to meet men. The pumpkin patch. The doughnut shop."

"I can see you're not taking this seriously. Let me do

a demonstration." She signaled the waitress. "Can we have some of those churros, please?"

If the waitress thought it strange Ava was asking for dessert before they'd even been served their entrées, she didn't show it.

Ava returned her attention to him. "Have you eaten one of these? They're delicious. Sugar and cinnamon. Mmm."

The way she said *mmm* with such a level of carnal enjoyment made his stomach clench.

A moment later the waitress dropped off a platter of churros, as well as a basket of chips, salsa and queso.

"Cinnamon is another scent men respond to on a primal level. Plus the food has the added bonus of being somewhat phallic." Her voice had turned husky, as if her very words aroused her.

She cleared her throat, her green eyes never leaving his.

"I think it's most effective when a woman teases her face with the food a bit, running it along her chin. Her lips. Makes men think of a woman running her lips along his—"

Her words didn't drift off. He cut them off in his mind. He knew exactly what seeing a woman with something like a churro, seeing Ava do with that churro, made him think. It made him think of her lips on his erection.

"The key is to keep the man in a steady state of semi-arousal at all times."

Semiarousal? He'd just gone from zero to performance status in about half a second.

She dropped the churro onto the platter. "You see? Food is one very important ingredient for sex. You show me a man whose mind doesn't immediately turn to a blow job at the sight of a woman eating a banana or carrot— I'll show you a man whose balls haven't dropped yet."

Or one who wasn't into women. He turned to face Ava, whose expression was teasing. "Okay, you have a point," he admitted, speaking around the lump in his throat.

She smiled, bit off the tip of the churro with gusto, then tipped it his way. "Bite?"

"No, thank you."

The scent of cinnamon drifted back to him. Was that the food or the woman? And more importantly, was she wearing it on purpose?

"Food-sharing is also very erotic. The significance more than likely dates back to when humans were in survival mode. To share your food literally meant to share your life. Now, eating from your lover's hand reveals an innate trust. All this academic talk, I'm not boring you am I?"

Hell, no. If the classes he'd taken in college had been half this interesting, he might have stayed to finish his degree. He shook his head.

"Good. Do you like churros, Ian?" her voice husky again and full of playful invitation.

He nodded.

Once more, she tipped the food in his direction. "See how sexy, almost carnal it can be to eat from my hand? It's especially effective if you've never kissed your partner."

She used the food to trace his bottom lip. He couldn't breathe. He couldn't do a thing.

"To have your lips touch where just moments ago hers had been. Her tongue, her saliva…it's like sharing a passionate kiss. A prelude of more to come."

He bit down on the food, tasting the sweetness. Tasting her. Satisfaction was light in the greenness of her eyes. And he felt as if he'd just bitten off more than he could chew….

6

KELSO. SO JEREMY had a last name. The Jeremy who should be in Oklahoma but was now apparently in her outer lobby. Miriam cleared her throat.

"Thanks, Rich. Give me about five minutes then send him in."

Miriam stood and smoothed the wrinkles from her skirt. Ahh, if only smoothing out the wrinkles of her life could be so easy. She was avoiding this person. Had done an admirable job of keeping him from her mind. Mostly. Why'd he have to show up?

The covers on her wall mocked her.

The Mistake You'll Always Regret

Forget Your Forbidden Fruit

Are You Replacing His Mother?

Miriam scowled at that last cover. Okay, she was being ridiculous. None of those headlines even had anything to do with dating younger men. There was no reason to panic. She was a grown woman, had responsibilities and lived up to her commitments.

So she'd had a one-night stand.

So her one-night stand had decided to show up unannounced. She could handle this. Handle it with style and grace and confidently explain to Jeremy that the one-night man did not linger.

Long-distance relationship?

Shoot. Why'd her mind have to wander in that direction?

There were rules about long-distance relationships and she'd made sure of it. She flipped to the review copy of the article she'd recommended for *The Rage*. The sidebar had a few "quick-read" suggestions.

Loving Your Long Distance and Keeping It that Way
1. Don't look for them to last.

Okay, really no problem there.

2. Make frequent-flier miles your best friend.

She had some just itching to be used.

3. Communicate clear expectations.

Obviously she'd already failed in that area, otherwise there wouldn't be a twentysomething man waiting for her in the outer lobby.

4. Be especially creative.

Actually, she and her twentysomething lover already had that down.

5. Remember—the odds are not in your favor.

Yes, but when had they been?

All excellent points of policy.

There was a brief knock on the door, and then Rich efficiently ushered Jeremy into her office, quickly closing the door behind him. And there he was. Jeremy of the now-known last name. Jeremy Kelso, who could rock her world eight times in a night.

Her breath hitched, and her hands grew clammy. She was disgusted with herself. Miriam Cole was about to fall into the worst cliché, and she allowed herself to be mentally sucked back into the past.

Suddenly, she was on that nearly-deserted, dusty-red highway in Oklahoma. Hot, tired and stranded. An old, beat-up truck had pulled up beside her.

For a moment she felt only sweet relief. She wouldn't die out in the middle of nowhere. Then every article in her magazine ever written about women alone and out in the middle of nowhere flashed through her mind. A car, let alone a pickup truck, happening upon her was far worse than being out here by herself.

"Need some help?" asked the lone occupant after he slowed to a stop.

Miriam flashed him what she knew worked on the dating scene as the polite brush-off smile. "No, no. I'm fine."

The man leaned across the seat, but his face was still hidden in the shadows. "I could give you a lift into town if you need it."

Get into the car of a complete stranger? What did she look like, an idiot? *This* was exactly how people got abducted. Killed.

"Thanks, but no," she told him firmly as she reached for her phone. Cell phones were excellent man-conversation blockers in the dating world. Surely it would serve the same function now.

"Oh, that won't work here. The mountains stop the signal."

Miriam turned away from the stranger and took a breath. Her ruse hadn't worked. She wasn't in her element here in the middle of nowhere. In Manhattan she knew how to take care of herself. But here she had no Mace and no cell phone. She felt practically helpless.

"Look, you're clearly in trouble. Hop in and I'll take you into town."

Miriam didn't hop into trucks. She glided elegantly into cars. With sophistication and great shoes. She took another deep breath and faced her would be rescuer or killer. "How far is it into town?"

"About five miles."

She sighed in relief. She jogged two miles in the park every day. "I can walk. Thanks again," she said, clearly a signal to the driver that his help wasn't needed and he could move on.

"Have a nice day," he offered, moved back in front of the wheel and put the truck in gear. He drove away with a kickup of dust.

Miriam slumped against her car. Okay, so probably

he wasn't a serial killer or anything bad, but that didn't mean a woman should be reckless with her safety. So she waited another five minutes then headed down the road, and vowed never to rent a car and trek in unfamiliar territory again.

Fifteen minutes into her journey, she spotted the truck a second time. Coming back towards her. Her stomach clenched and her legs tightened. There could be no reason for him to be back out here.

The driver was on her side and she could clearly see him. He'd pulled right up beside her on the wrong side of the road, and she glanced in his direction. In a bar, in a boardroom, she wouldn't have hesitated to give him her number. Dark hair, beautiful eyes…delicious smile. This was even more dangerous. She quickened her pace.

"I understand you not wanting to get into the car with a stranger, but I don't feel right about you walking into town by yourself. So I'll just follow along behind you."

She stopped and stared at him. "Let me get this straight. You're going to follow me into town…just to make sure I get there safe?"

With a nod, he did a three-point turn in the middle of the road and drove slowly behind her as she indeed walked all the way to town.

Her car had bailed on her. She'd been stranded and left without any way to contact the outside world…and yet Miriam had never felt safer.

And now, here in her office, Jeremy Kelso smiled at her. That same smile that had won her over in the garage as she waited for her rental to be towed into town. That same smile that made her open up and talk with him over dinner. That same smile that made naughty promises that his body kept all through the night.

Suddenly, she didn't feel so safe anymore.

MOST OF IAN'S MEALS were caught on the road or out in the field. He lived on beef jerky and cold cans of lima beans. So, when he had the opportunity to sit down and enjoy a well-prepared meal he enjoyed it to the fullest.

Mendoza's had the kind of casual atmosphere that instantly made him relax. From the brightly colored wooden chairs with straw seats to the scent of freshly made flour tortillas in the air, he suddenly missed his time spent south of the border. He'd loved it all. The bustle of Mexico City. The warm, tropical breezes off the coast.

Ian sat straighter in his chair. Maybe that importance-of-food-to-men stuff Ava was talking about wasn't half-baked, because despite being in a constant state of sexual frustration since she'd stroked that churro around her mouth, he was having a great time.

She sat across from him, animated and energized, discussing all the people she'd met. Her blond hair, now dry, moved around her face as she spoke. The meal was leisurely and he was glad she continued to chat about her experiences once their food arrived.

Like him, Ava had traveled all over the world, but her stories seemed far more interesting than his. His natural reporter's instincts were to keep her talking. And the heat he'd felt since she'd opened that door to him wearing paint and a smile finally simmered down to a low burn.

"I think the scarf dance is one of my favorites. The woman spends hours circling her body with the material."

He'd probably never get this story out of his head. His travels hadn't taken him to places where women adorned themselves only with scarves. But instead of some faceless, nameless woman covered solely in ribbons, he pictured only the woman sitting across from him.

Ava's green eyes darkened. "Then she slowly unwinds each scarf from her body and binds her new husband's body with the material. His arms above his head. His legs together at the ankles, knee and thighs."

The scarf-removal thing he could get into…being tied up by a woman…not so much.

Ava smiled. "I can see you don't think much of the ceremony. But the Urmanian men were fierce warriors, often scarred from battle. A young bride might be frightened of her new husband and afraid of what was to happen between them. Most of these marriages were arranged between families, and the bride probably had never seen her new husband before their wedding ceremony."

"So wouldn't stripping in front of a man you've never met be scary?"

"Well, the girls practice the ceremony for many months, so that takes away any performance nerves. Plus, the whole point of the binding is to make the new bride comfortable. There's something very sensual about a big, strong man, a man who could easily overpower you, and bend you to his will…"

Her words drifted off, and she sucked on her lower

lip. Was that a tell? He hadn't spotted one glitch in this woman's "sex is sex" facade. Her full lips were parted, and there was a far-away look in her eyes.

Was the woman who had greeted him half-naked and covered in paint, the woman who could converse about sex, phallic symbols and smells that broke a man's will…did the idea of tying a man up make her pause? His stomach clenched as he waited to hear what she'd say. He might just be willing to consider letting her tie him up if he got to see her in that loincloth and paint again.

"Anyway, it's heady thinking about him allowing you to tie him up. Explore his body. Learn the power your body can have over his," she told him, her voice lower and reminding him of a warm wave washing over his skin.

That simmer he'd been operating under turned to boiling once more. He shifted in his seat, trying to relieve some of the pressure in his jeans.

Did she do it on purpose? Turn him on like that?

The sensual softening of her eyes disappeared and she shrugged, returning her attention to her food.

Ian scrutinized Ava as she spread guacamole onto a flat tortilla. She looked innocent enough, but she had to know. Had to know that her words made him think of her slowly taking off her clothes in front of him. Letting her bind him. Feeling her stroke him.

"The binding is an ancient art that's quite beautiful. I think it would make for some great visuals for the book," she said, her tone all business now. "It's interesting how beliefs manifest themselves. The Urmanian culture did not believe a strong, healthy baby could come from unions where the woman did not enjoy sex. The man wanted his wife to feel only pleasure in the marriage bed."

Hell, what man didn't want to see a woman feel pleasure? There was never a sight as sexy as seeing a woman come.

She pointed her fork at him. "In fact, there is some research that suggests when a woman has an orgasm she conceives more easily."

This had to be, without a doubt, the weirdest conversation he'd ever had. He'd usually bolt at the first hint of the word *conception*.

Ava speared a bite of seared pepper from the fajita skillet onto her fork. "Red and green chilies are great for sex."

Was he going to jerk every time the professor said the word *sex?*

"The chilies get your circulation going. I was thinking we could include recipes that had a lot of aphrodisiacal properties. There are several that don't have long accompanying stories, but would be fun to include."

Yeah, he'd like to hear what this woman's idea of fun was. "Like what?" he asked.

"Celery. Good for all your muscles. Did you know that the ancient Tragrils actually devoted celery to their god of sex and of hell?"

He felt the irony.

"Sex is all around us, has been from the very beginnings of culture." Ava shrugged. "You could probably point at anything in this restaurant and we can relate it somehow to sex."

This he'd like to see. "How about that guacamole you've devoured?" he suggested, indicating the now-empty serving dish.

Ava sat back against her chair as if in thought. "Guacamole is made from avocados. Which is also the Aztec word for a certain part of the male anatomy."

"This restaurant."

"Sometimes in Mexico, a rope is placed around the neck of the bride and groom. Physical binding of a newly married couple is quite common in many cultures."

He was kind of liking this naughtier version of the six-degrees-of-separation game. Ava was right—she didn't have to go too far for her examples. Ian picked up his knife to cut off another bite of enchilada.

"This knife," he suggested.

"Oh, that's easy. In Nordic history, when a father had a marriageable daughter, he'd place an empty knife sheath on her belt or around her waist. Interested suitors would place their knife in the empty case. That evokes all kinds of images, doesn't it?"

It certainly did. Ian leaned forward. "How about you, Dr. Simms?"

A tiny smile tugged at her top lip. "Women with Ph.D.s are twice as likely to have a one-night stand as those with a B.A."

Which made him wonder about *Doctor* Simms.

That's when it hit him. The humor, the passion the respect she had for all these people she'd met and cultures she'd studied…none of that was in her book. It was dry and dull.

Which she clearly was not.

Her passion, her personality, Ava…that's what would sell this book. Every word, every image had to evoke the enthusiasm and excitement and utter zest that was Ava.

This wasn't going to be just reviewing her notes and taking a few pictures…he'd need to spend real time with her. Earlier he couldn't wait to get out of this assignment. He'd been restless to set off again, to do his own story, live life on the edge as he wanted.

But now something was different. That edgy impatient restlessness led him to Ava, which led him to wanting to stay. And that was the first thing that had ever scared him.

7

IAN PAID FOR DINNER. It had been a struggle knowing what to do. He'd run across some women in the past who'd felt it was insulting for a man to pay for their meal. Unlike his mother, who'd raised him to believe men paid for everything. That, in fact, *all* men should pay.

Ava just seemed to be clueless about what to do when the check arrived. Something he found oddly...endearing. She nodded to herself when he placed his credit card on the bill, as if mentally making notes of his actions.

Now they were walking back to her warehouse apartment. The foot traffic along the canal had increased so their pace slowed. He wasn't much for leisurely strolls, but Ava was definitely the kind who stopped and smelled the flowers. And she could probably tell him some new tormenting fact about how women strung them together to frame their nipples, or rubbed the blooms along a man's...

What the hell was happening to him? Sure, he'd been covering some out-of-control stories for a while and it had been a long time since he'd been in the company of the opposite sex, but his physical reaction toward Ava was unlike anything he'd experienced before. It was as if every word from her kissable lips and every stretch of her sensuous body was specifically designed to make him think of nothing but stroking her lips with his. Caressing her skin. Palming her breasts. Making love to her fast. Or slowly. Whatever. However. Just as long as the action between the sheets lasted for hours.

That's when it hit him. It *was* all designed. Her every move. Her every supposedly subtle, yet utterly sensual maneuver had been intended to keep his mind on one thing and one thing only. Sex. Not that it was a hard task, but to have his easily led thoughts manipulated in that direction… He stopped walking and just stared at her. He was irritated and impressed all at the same time.

Ava stopped and turned around to look at him. "Everything okay?" she asked, the scent of cinnamon slyly hitting his nose as her hair swirled around her head.

"You're using the book stuff on me."

She crooked an eyebrow. "Is that what I'm doing?" she asked, her voice innocent. Her eyes…nothing close.

He shook his head ruefully. Knowing she'd played him for the last hour didn't detract from how sexy she was. How sexy he found her.

"Was it working?" she asked, her tones now sensual and low. And his body responded once again.

"No," he told her.

Her lips curved into a smile. "Good," she said with a nod. "That was only level-one stuff anyway. I'll just have to ramp it up some."

Hell, he was going to die.

JEREMY LOOKED AROUND her office and whistled. "You didn't tell me you were in charge. Impressive."

Yeah, well, there isn't a lot of talking involved when a man's tongue is in your mouth.

Miriam schooled her features to look cool and professional. "What a surprise to see you here, Jeremy."

He quickly shifted his glance her way, the smile on his face fading. "But not a good surprise, huh?" he asked, his disappointment obvious in his voice.

He caught on fast. Not so surprising since he'd so easily interpreted her every quick intake of breath or delicious sigh in bed and understood exactly what she wanted.

She moved so that she sat behind her desk. She needed that barrier between them. "I wasn't expecting to see you ever again."

Now all traces of that sexy open smile of his vanished. "That was pretty obvious by the way you left the next morning without a trace."

She would ignore the hurt she saw in his eyes. *Get this over quickly. No need to prolong anything.* "Then why are you here?" she asked.

He slowly moved toward her desk, drawing her eyes to his tall lean body. She'd stroked and kissed every part of that provocative body of his. Earlier she'd chalked up her momentary loss of judgment where Jeremy was concerned to the strange situation.

She had been on vacation.

She'd been stranded.

He'd played the role of knight coming to her rescue. Of course she'd fallen into his arms. She could still feel the heat of him as he'd brought her a drink in the town's garage. He'd made her laugh because he'd placed a straw in one of those fluid-replenishing sports drinks.

"Thought you might be thirsty," he'd said. And she was. Oh, she'd been thirsty for just what Jeremy had to give. He'd sat with her the whole time the mechanics worked on her car.

Listened to her and laughed at her stories over dinner.

He'd offered to walk her to the door of her hotel room. Just to make sure she was safe. She was only going to thank him and wish him good-night. But she'd been hungry to know what his lips tasted like.

In fact, she was still hungry and still thirsty. Her breath shallowed. Her heartbeat quickened.

"Thought by now you might have changed your mind about seeing me again," he said. His voice was a sensual caress against her skin. Just a hint of an accent. His blue eyes willed her to rethink her decision to not see him again.

Of course she'd changed her mind. She'd gone back and forth about ten thousand times.

Look away. But her eyes fell across the magazine covers.

Go For It
Take Charge
Do What You've Been Dying To Do

Miriam stood, her breasts only an inch from Jeremy's chest. He smelled good. Like fresh air, lime and hungry man. Hungry for her. Good to know she'd left an impression on him.

She ran her fingertips up his arm, and his eyes heated. "How about dinner?" she asked.

He lifted an eyebrow. "How about takeout?"

AVA SMILED AT IAN. She should probably feel bad about torturing this man. At least she was hoping it was torture. Strangely enough, all her stealth-seduction practices hadn't been so easy on her. Playing the subtle flirt took a lot of energy. And it was hell on her body. She'd spent that last half hour in first-stage arousal.

She turned and began walking again, knowing he'd be beside her. She liked that he'd caught on so quickly. She liked smart men.

"You don't even feel guilty about trying to drive me nearly insane this whole time?" he asked, as he matched his stride to hers.

"Would kind of miss the mark if I were."

Earlier today, she'd been concerned about this project. Greeting this man nearly naked and covered in paint had clearly been the wrong direction this morning. But she'd managed to work it to her advantage.

"You're taking this book seriously now though."

She saw him smile. "Oh, yeah. Was I that obvious in your apartment?"

"It was very clear you didn't want to be anywhere near this project. Not your style?"

He shook his head, a dimple forming in his cheek. "No. But I warn you, you won't be able to fool me so easily next time."

She smiled. Liking that about him, hoping he'd keep

working under that assumption. "Good. I wouldn't want you easy."

They walked together silently, enjoying the stroll around the canal. Although she'd been in her new home for a week, she hadn't taken the time to explore the beautiful Bricktown area. The flowers and trees surrounding the canal were lovely, and quite surprising to find in the middle of a busy downtown area. The sun was setting, and the various businesses had turned on their lights, many reflecting in the water. A family of ducks paddled by, swimming toward two children tossing bits of tortilla into the water.

"It's pretty here," she said.

Ian shrugged. "Sure."

Her instincts about this man were right. He was wound tight. "You know, in ancient England, men would collect flowers and wind them into garlands. They'd spend hours examining the blooms, making sure each petal was perfect. Then with great enthusiasm, the knight would place his unique creation on top of his beloved's head."

Ian made a scoffing noise. "That sounds like something a bunch of women cooked up and *told* men they enjoyed doing."

"You seem awfully cynical about the opposite sex." Now this was interesting. Could this be an actual insight into the man? Good, this could be something to use later. For the book or on the man, she wasn't quite sure which.

He stopped and turned toward her. They were under a bridge, and the lights cast amber shadows around his face. "We're talking about knights, right? Armor, lances, raiding castles. You might want to go back and research the whole flower thing."

"It's well-documented."

His lip crooked upward. "Men…spending hours selecting flowers? I don't even give that much thought to my socks. And I'm wearing them. What probably happened was that the knight was on his way back to the armory after a hard day's battle keeping everyone safe. That's when he saw some slacker dumbass knight with a bunch of flowers heading toward his woman. He couldn't let that happen, so found some vendor with a cart selling flowers."

"Oh, really," Ava said, flashing him her best skeptical look, the one she'd seen her college professors use a thousand times. All the while she tried to hide her smile.

"The vendor was probably so bored from trying to sell flowers to a bunch of dirty knights that he fidgeted those blooms into a string, or 'garland' if you will."

She couldn't stop her laugh. "Did you just use air quotes?"

"Shh. You're messing up my story. And I'm on a roll because here's the best part. He speeds past this other knight, and then *tells* his woman he spent hours selecting the right blooms for this twisted-up mess. He even has her thinking garland is attractive. That women actually want garland. Desire it."

"No, your theory doesn't float because now he sets up a standard that he has to beat and that all his sons and grandsons have to meet. They have to actually collect flowers and make garland."

"Not necessarily, because he passes along the DNA that allows his heirs to make up their own BS stories with enough convincibility that women think they're hot."

"*Convincibility* is not a word."

Ian held up his hands and took a few steps back. That sexy dimple appeared in his cheek again. "Hey, no need to get testy just because I blew your whole men-and-flowers scenario out of the water."

Ava laughed. "Are you going to be this doubtful about all the customs I'm putting forth?"

"I'm just glad I'm here to make sure you don't send the men down the wrong path." Then with a wink, he turned and began walking again.

"Just so long as you know you're wrong," she told him as she joined him. She could spot her apartment now, and despite knowing how wrong he was, she was interested to hear what other theories he was going to try and debunk.

Fifteen minutes later, Ava emerged from her bedroom, barefoot and with a box full of scrapbooks and photo albums. She'd spent time in so many cultures where shoes were not worn, she felt confined in straps of leather, no matter how cute.

She found Ian staring outside her large picture window at the canal below. One of the yellow boats floated along the river. This was her first opportunity to really study him unnoticed. He was a man who observed everything. Probably from his journalistic training. He'd notice her examining him. More than likely he'd use it to his advantage.

Strange. She didn't think they were at war or anything. But there was definitely a tension between them. Both of them were wanting to win. Win at what, she didn't know.

He looked good, relaxed in the khaki pants and polo shirt. Ian was a lot different from the usual men in her circle. Who was she kidding? He was totally different from the academic types. Professors had a reputation for being boring and staid, but really that was an unfair stereotype. Usually they were just so focused on one subject they could talk of little else.

Ian seemed like a man who could focus, too. Only the difference was that he could focus on lots of different things at once. She liked that he cared enough about his sister that he would clearly involve himself in something he thought he'd loathe because she asked him to. She knew her brother would do the same for her.

She also liked how he quickly dropped his bias toward her project and even challenged her to think about this book in ways she hadn't thought of before. A man who challenged her mind was definitely very sexy.

Her body reacted, and she closed her eyes for a moment to enjoy the sensation. She'd be making love to this man. Ava didn't know when, but the fact that it would happen was a certainty and she planned to savor the delicious buildup and tension that existed between a man and a woman before they succumbed to the call of their bodies.

So she'd admire Ian's body. And his mind. For now. As for later...

"It's a great view, isn't it?" she asked.

Ian turned, and his eyes darkened when he saw her. "It certainly is," he said.

She smiled, then turned toward the brown couch in the middle of the large front area of her apartment. She patted the seat beside her, indicating she wanted him to sit down.

He tossed aside a decorative pillow and sat. Once again she took some time to appreciate the moment. His bigness, his strength, the heat emanating from his skin. Nature had made her desire these things in a man. Who was she to deny it?

There was a principle she wanted to impress in her book, and that was showing women and men how to appreciate the strength and power of the feminine. Somewhere along the way, that positive reception seemed to have gotten lost. A whole wealth of pleasure and completion awaited the senses when male and female united.

She opened her photo album. "My photography is pretty crude, but this is an interesting union ceremony. Eligible males and females are lined up. Men on one side. Women on the other." She pointed to the rows of people, their muscles tense with nerves, their expressions anxious.

She turned the page, and pointed to a building made of bamboo and leaves. "The elders emerge from a spirit hut after several days of fasting and prayer. Then they join a couple based on what the spirit tells them."

Ian shuddered. "That's awful. No wonder they look as if they're about to face death. The spirit could give a man some woman who's constantly asking what he's thinking about. Or invites him to a musical."

Not taking the bait, mister. She shrugged instead. "It seems to work. Separation doesn't happen very often, although after a year, the couple can petition the elders to dissolve the union. But they have to wait another two years for another ceremony. They're only performed every three years. And two years is a long time to wait and be alone." She turned the page to show newly formed couples holding hands.

She'd spent two years off and on with this particular tribe, one of the last of its kind. "Look, here are some of their children a year later." She loved looking at the proud daddies holding new infants at the naming ceremony.

"But to spend your entire life with someone you don't even know. To put that kind of faith in someone else to choose for you."

"Almost every culture in the world at one time or another has had arranged marriages. It's as if the older people don't put a lot of faith in the judgment of the young," she said with a laugh.

Then she focused her attention on Ian's brown eyes. "In fact, choosing one's own mate is relatively new."

If Ian didn't pick up the message she was communicating with her eyes, he just wasn't getting it. A woman could do a lot of silent talking with her eyes. Dozens of cultures never allowed women and men to talk until introduced, but women had adapted over time so the men they weren't supposed to talk to knew exactly what they were saying. For some societies, it was the language of the fan. In others it was with the eyes. And Ava had learned from the best.

Oh, a man might think he's the aggressor in approaching a woman, but he'd probably been picking up the subtle cues and hints the woman had been throwing his way all along. Men in any culture didn't like to be turned down.

The stiffening of Ian's shoulders proved he'd caught on to the message she was sending through her gaze. What would he do now? Would he take her up on it?

"Well, it probably beats speed dating," Ian said after a downward glance at her lips before he returned his attention to the photo album. His brown eyes were tinged with desire.

She racked her brain trying to find a reference, and failed. "What's speed dating?"

"You haven't heard of it?" he asked, his voice incredulous.

She shook her head.

"Actually, it's not much different than this tradition here, the men and women are lined up, but then the men move from woman to woman in a row, spending about five minutes with each. Then both the men and women mark on a card whether they want to see a particular person again. If both people mark yes, then the organizers will exchange their information."

"Wow. I can't decide if that's a really great idea or a really bad one. Sexual attraction does happen almost instantaneously."

"Internet dating is even worse."

"Internet dating?"

Ian turned on the couch so that he faced her. "You haven't heard of that, either?"

For some reason, she was feeling almost defensive. "Most of my life has been spent out of the country."

"But you went to college."

"Sure, but my course work took me right back in the field mainly. I only lived one semester in the residence halls, but spent most of that time in the library."

"What about before that?"

"With my mom and dad at sites."

"So, you've never been to a prom, never cruised, never hung out at the food court of the mall?"

She shrugged. "What's the big deal about that?"

His breath came out in a huff, ruffling his hair. "You know so much about cultures all around the world, but you're clueless about your own."

She blinked up at him in surprise. "I'm certainly no shy virgin. I've dated plenty."

"What, other students? That's easy. I'm talking about meeting people. That's hard. You're going to be selling this book to people who *have* hung around the grocery store looking for others buying single-portion meals. I think you need to experience a little of their life to be able to write for them."

This sounded like another session of him debunking her theories. It also sounded very exciting. "Okay, I'm game. When do we start?"

"Right now. Where's your phone book?"

"Under the cabinet by the phone. Why?"

Ian shot off her couch and grabbed her Yellow Pages.

He ran his finger along the page as he spoke. "Brick-town is a happening place. Surely there's a— Found it."

"Found what?"

"Club Escape. Ava Simms, you're about to have your first experience in a singles' bar."

8

MIRIAM USHERED Jeremy out of her office quickly. They'd almost made it to the bank of elevators when her assistant rushed toward her.

"Thank God I caught you. It's…your mother."

Miriam's shoulders sagged. She closed her eyes briefly, dragging in a breath. Jeremy obviously sensed something because he took a step toward her, and placed a comforting hand on her shoulder. The tip-off must have been the alarmed glances between her and Rich. Or more likely, her body's natural bracing stance for the emotional combat sure to come.

Whatever it was, she appreciated the gesture. His hand, warm and solid, actually felt comforting and well, nice.

Rich cut a glance toward Jeremy, then back to her. "I could tell your mom you've already left for the day."

Like the former Mrs. Cole would believe that. When had Miriam ever left work—she looked down at her watch—before seven? She shook her head. "No, she'll just track me down on my cell."

Rich nodded. "I'll tell her you'll be right there. She'll be on line two."

Miriam turned toward Jeremy. "I'm sorry about this, but it's something I can't get out of. You don't have to stay—"

He shook his head and smiled. "No, I'll wait," he said, as if there was never any question that he would.

She raised a brow. "This may take a while. In fact, it probably will. You could go back to your hotel. Leave your number, and I'll call you—"

"Miriam, it's okay," he said, his voice reassuring. His blue eyes supportive.

With a tight smile, she turned and headed back to her office, sighing heavily.

Miriam's mom was what some people would call a gold digger. She was smart, pretty, talented and above all—ruthless. Instead of using all that power to carve a career out for herself, she latched on to rich and success-ful men.

Miriam and Ian's father had been her first husband, but she'd left him, as well as the rest of her family, to marry a rich rancher in Montana. Today she was married to some obscure painter and living overseas, no doubt funding his work now that she was a very wealthy woman.

About five years ago, Miriam had finally contacted her. They'd been doing an article on what drove women to marry for status and position rather than love, and her mother had offered up several enlightening quotes. Anonymously, of course.

Miriam doubted she'd ever connect with the woman who'd given her life, but she understood some of what drove her. Since that interview her mother called her on a regular basis. Miriam had tried to assign all sorts of reasons for the contact: Janice felt guilty for leaving her children or she wanted to connect with her only blood relations, but she really suspected that Janice liked trying on the mother role every once in a while. Hence her concern about Ian's current occupation.

Miriam returned to her office, and picked up her extension. "Darling, you cannot believe what they've been doing to poor Raoul."

Miriam had never met her mother's latest, and it was hard to work up any sympathy for the man—other than for the fact that he was married to her mother.

"They are canceling his showing. The poor man is having painter's block. He can't help it."

She'd heard of writer's block, but painter's? "Well, mother, it would be hard to have a showing without any paintings."

"Oh, Miriam, if they weren't hassling him so much about his new vision, he wouldn't be having these problems to begin with. He…"

Miriam opened her top desk drawer and pulled out a doodle pad she reserved solely for phone conversations with her mother. She'd never used a doodle pad before, preferring short conversation that encapsulated in five minutes or less whatever pressing business needed to be dealt with. But Rich had purchased one for her after he'd found her mad scribblings all over her desk calendar. He'd not been pleased.

Twenty minutes later, she found herself walking

back to the elevator. Wrung out and fully expecting to see an empty lobby. Then she spotted the man leaning against the wall, an anxious expression in his blue eyes. Her mouth went dry and her heart began to race.

"Are you okay?" he asked, his voice deeper than usual, laced with concern.

She glanced up, meeting his gaze, surprised to hear genuine worry behind his words. The skin around his eyes was tight, and his whole big body seemed tense. The muscles of his arms bunched, as though he was ready to engage in battle.

Battle for her?

The tension in her back eased. "You waited," she said, not realizing until that moment that she'd secretly hoped he would, but hadn't really expected it.

A flash of annoyance shot into his eyes. "Of course I waited."

Something happened to her in that moment. Miriam Cole no longer felt so alone. It felt almost natural to have him at her side. She gave him a tentative smile. "I'm fine. I just want to get out of here."

He punched the down button. "I know about mothers."

"Not like mine," she said.

Jeremy gave her a sympathetic hand squeeze. Among her friends, when the topic of bad parents arose, a competition of sorts began. Whose mother had been the worst? Whose father had the most "other" families? But Jeremy did none of those things. Instead he gave her an easy yet comprehensive form of acknowledgment. And he listened.

She gave him a sideways glance as they waited for the elevator. He'd gotten a haircut since she'd last seen him. Had he done that for her? The thought that he might have warmed her from the inside, even though she kind of liked brushing his dark hair out of his eyes.

He was even better than she'd remembered. And lying in the dark in her big, lonely bed for the last few weeks, she'd recalled him looking pretty damn good.

The downward-facing arrow above the elevator lit up and a bell pinged as the elevator doors whooshed open. She followed him inside and punched the lobby button, and the doors closed.

In a stride and a half, Jeremy was at her side, and tugging her into his arms.

His lips came down on hers. For a moment she was too surprised to respond. Then it all came flooding back. The passion. The heat. The hungry wanting Jeremy evoked in her. She'd missed the fervor, that excitement so much. She'd missed him.

Miriam circled her fingers in the loops of Jeremy's jeans and yanked. Hard. But she didn't care. She wanted to feel the solidness of his chest against her breasts. Feel the hardness of his erection pushing into her gray silk business skirt.

With a groan, Jeremy backed her against the wall and his hands cupped her breasts, touching and stroking her in a way that made her wet and hot.

He'd remembered what she'd liked. Just the way she'd liked it.

The rapid descent of the express elevator slowed.

They'd be reaching the lower floors now. With obvious reluctance, Jeremy's mouth left hers. His ragged breathing filled the car, as he rested his forehead against hers.

"I've thought of nothing else but that," he said. And Miriam felt another jolt of tingles at his words. She'd never melted against a guy in her life. But here she was, practically liquefying herself against the man.

Her dry mouth hadn't recovered from the sight of him propped up against the wall waiting for her. And now she had to deal with the lack of his lips.

The elevator door opened, and they stepped out. Calm, cool and with a respectable distance apart of almost two feet. No one passing by would suspect the heat that had fired up the elevator only moments before.

Jeremy drew her toward the glass doors that led outside, his hand warm on her lower back.

They walked together in silence. But for the first time, she didn't feel the urge to fill it, rack her brain for some tidbit of information that would keep the conversation going. Actually, she kind of liked the calm between them.

The calm before the storm.

Because they both knew the minute they were alone, the passion between then would take off full force. There should be some sort of awkward tension right now. Some sort of preintercourse nerves or reserve. Instead she felt an affinity with the man whose body heat penetrated her blouse directly to her skin, and couldn't they walk through this lobby any faster?

Finally they made it outside and Miriam began to flag down a taxi.

"Do you want to walk?" Jeremy asked, his face turning a little green.

Her arm lowered, and she turned toward him. Miriam tried not to look at him as if he was crazy. She really did. But it was cold. She was in heels. It was—

Then she remembered he'd never been to New York before. She could point out a few sights. He could rub her feet afterwards.

"Are you wanting to see a few landmarks?" What happened to the hungry guy from her office? The one who didn't want to wait for a meal in a restaurant to have her?

"You think I drove all this way just to see Manhattan?"

"You drove?"

He nodded.

"All the way from Oklahoma."

He nodded again.

Forget takeout. She'd take him. Then afterwards, they'd order in.

And yet he still made no move toward the taxi.

Wait a minute. He looked about as uneasy as she'd felt alone and isolated on that lonely stretch of country highway.

That had been his element.

New York was hers. And she knew what every out-of-towner commented on after a visit. She stared in his direction. "The traffic getting to you?"

He shrugged. "What's with all the honking?"

She reached for his arm, and tugged him toward the cab. "Come on, big guy. This time I'll protect you."

Ava did an Internet search to find out what to wear to a nightclub and fifteen minutes later emerged from her bedroom hoping she'd fit in with the natives. She was usually a lot more prepared than this, spending hours researching adornment and attire.

By the fire behind Ian's eyes, her choice of black miniskirt, sparkly tank and sheer long-sleeved over-shirt hit the mark. Going heavy on the eyeliner and sheer lip gloss felt strange, but she went with the advice in an article she'd found in one of Cole Publishing's own magazines, *Dress To Be Noticed.*

"I won't stand out, will I?" she asked.

Ian nodded. Slowly. "That will do," he said, his voice slow. He crooked his elbow.

Unfamiliar with the gesture, she quickly figured out she was supposed to wind her own arm through his, appreciating the solid strength of his body.

"Technically, you're supposed to want to stand out. You're trying to attract men," he said with little enthusiasm.

Ava tilted her head. "Okay to stand out. Got it."

Like most of the attractions at Bricktown, the nightclub was on the canal, and it took only a few minutes to walk there from her apartment.

She heard the pounding synthesized beat of music long before she turned the corner to the Club Escape. Two large black doors bore the word *Escape* in bold, neon blue. Ian escorted her into a darkened hallway, shrouded in pale blue light. After flashing her ID and paying the cover charge, they followed the music down the hallway.

Lights overhead pulsing in beat with the music illuminated dozens of people dancing on a large floor. She'd participated in many types of ritualistic dancing, but nothing ever this…free-form. She preferred her customs a bit more scripted than this.

Ian indicated a grouping of purple couches and she followed him as he led the way, pushing through the crowd.

A waitress quickly stopped at their table and asked for their drink orders.

Ava leaned over to Ian. "What's the normal drink for a woman to order?"

Rather than reply, he told the waitress, "She'll have an appletini. I'll have a beer. Domestic."

"Draft or bottle?"

"Bottle."

"What's an appletini?" she asked as soon as the waitress left.

Ian shrugged. "Hell if I know. It's what my sister always orders."

She sat in silence beside him just digesting the sights and sounds around her. The smell of various perfumes and colognes scented the air. People grouped and clustered everywhere, trying to make conversation and laughing. There was an interesting anthropological study in this experience she was sure. Too bad she hadn't brought her camera.

DAMN ALL THE LOCKS on her door. It took too long for Miriam to enter her apartment. She could have been using tongs to hold her keys her fingers felt so useless.

Her heart raced in anticipation. She couldn't wait to get Jeremy alone and inside her apartment.

Finally. Her door swung open, and then Jeremy took over. Except he was even slower. She wanted hard and fast. And eight times in a night.

Instead he closed the door, locked it and gently pushed her against it. He cupped her face, and she met his blue gaze. He stroked her bottom lip with his thumb.

"I've dreamed about these lips," he told her. His voice gruff and full of desire.

He traced the line of her jaw. Slid his fingers down the line of her neck. A small smile touched his mouth as he found her pulse point. He leaned over and placed a light kiss there. An innocent kiss. One that would look almost chaste until he added the tip of his tongue. Then her pulse really began to hammer.

"Seeing how much you want me makes me hurt not to be inside you," he said with a groan against her skin.

"Then why are you being so slow?" Her breasts ached for his touch.

Jeremy straightened, his expression turning serious. "Because I told myself if I was lucky enough to be with you again, I wouldn't rush things like a horny jerk."

"I liked horny and rushed."

A wicked little grin appeared on his face. "You'll like this more."

Then his hands moved. He slid her jacket from her shoulders, making the simple act a carnal caress. She wanted his mouth on hers, his tongue at the base of her neck as he undressed her. Like before.

But now, his eyes never left hers as he began to unbutton her blouse. How intimate it felt to have him slowly undress her in the stark light of her entry.

His expression was a mask of tight concentration. His shoulders strained and tense. Jeremy Kelso was perfect. Beautiful.

Before, in Oklahoma, they'd raced to the bed. Two people in the heady throes of passion who couldn't get their clothes off fast enough.

His deliberate movements now were far more frustratingly sexy. He clearly was a man who'd thought of nothing else but undressing her slowly, and he planned on enjoying every moment now that he had the chance. Jeremy's eyes darkened, but never left hers. Although she couldn't hold his gaze as he caressed her nipples poking at her bra.

She moaned when he cupped her breasts, molding them with his hands. "Take off my bra," she said, her voice low and needy.

She hadn't wanted to be naked with a man this much since…since the last time she'd been with Jeremy. How he could make her breasts ache without taking off the material that separated his skin from hers, she'd never know.

He finally removed her lacy blue underwire. "I've waited so long to see you. Wanted you for so long."

The cool air of her apartment did nothing to soothe her need for his touch. And once again he was taking too long. Miriam opened her mouth to demand he touch her. She was done being teased.

She sucked in a breath when she opened her eyes and saw his expression. Jeremy looked at her body with intense appreciation. She watched as his breathing grew more irregular. Spotted his pulse beating wildly at his temple. Witnessing the effect she had on him made her feel strong.

"You're so beautiful," he said.

Miriam reached for his hands and unhurriedly placed them on her breasts. "Then touch me," she urged.

She didn't need to hide her lonely desire for him behind the quick, all-consuming passion. Miriam suddenly wanted to savor this, too.

She'd been imagining, dreaming, thinking of being with him as much as he had dreamed of being with her.

He kissed her then. Carnal and hungry. She opened for his tongue, the taste of him so memorable. So wanted. She twisted her hips until she cradled his erection. Her body demanding more from him. Offering more.

One quick weekend. It should have been nothing more, but she'd missed this. Missed him. The slightly rough texture of his cheek. His familiar masculine scent. The heat of his breath on her skin.

His lips left hers, running down her neck, down the swell of her breasts, stopping to give an erotic kiss to her breasts. Then lower still.

He sank to his knees, his fingers seeking out the waistband of her skirt and finding the zipper. The swish of her zipper being pulled down would be branded on her memory as one of the sexiest sounds she'd ever heard. Her thighs began to tremble.

"You make me feel so good, Jeremy." He pulled her stockings, panties and skirt down her legs all in one move. The man had talent. She stood before him naked. Warmth flooded between her legs. Miriam grew slicker with wanting. Jeremy's fingertips lightly guided up her calves.

"The whole weekend together, and not once did I kiss you here. How could I have missed that?"

The idea of his mouth, his tongue on the most intimate part of her body, made her knees shake in delicious expectation. It was hard for her to swallow. "We were busy doing other things," she reminded him, desperately trying not to sound so…desperate.

She watched as he smiled. "True."

Then he looked at the curls between her thighs. "I'm not missing this time."

He tenderly gripped her thighs, worked his shoulders between her legs. Then she felt the warmth of his mouth. He stroked her with his tongue, gently at first, as though she was fragile. As though he wanted to tease her and make her ache for more.

She shivered as he caressed and explored her with his tongue, seeming to want to learn every curve of her, the taste of her.

Her head fell back, and she moaned at how good he felt. How good he made her feel. Her knees wanted to buckle, but no way would she allow herself to break contact.

He circled her clit with his mouth, getting so close, but never fully finding the source of her most intense pleasure. Then he was there, licking her, sucking her. The thrilling pressure inside her deepened. She wanted…she needed…

Miriam's orgasm rushed her. An amazing release that went on and on and on. Jeremy saw that it did.

Finally, the pounding subsided. Her wobbly legs could hold her no longer, and she began to sink to the tile floor. Jeremy stood, bringing her up with him. Then he did something no man had ever done before. He swooped her up into the strength of his arms.

The sensation of being carried by him should have been corny. But she almost reveled in how cherished he made her feel. No one had ever made her feel so naughty and prized all at the same time. Naughty because all she could think of was that she wanted to give him as good as he was giving her.

"Where's your bedroom?" he asked, his voice gruff and tight with need.

"Down the hall, second door."

Jeremy didn't set her down when he reached her bedroom, he carried her all the way to the bed. Her breathing hitched as he let her body slide down the firmness of his until she sat on the mattress.

"Take my clothes off me," Jeremy told her. Miriam scooted to the head of the bed, and snapped on the bedside light. She wanted to see all of him.

Something in his eyes flickered for just a moment. Something wanting and almost vulnerable flashed there before it vanished. Replaced by desire.

Miriam slipped off the bed and took a leisurely tour around him. If he thought she was simply going to remove his clothes, he was wrong. She planned to enjoy this. Halting at his back, she tugged the T-shirt from his jeans. She ran her hand across his shoulders, loving the play of his muscles under her fingertips.

She went up his back with her breasts, her nipples hardening against the smooth heat of his skin.

"I like the way you take off a man's clothes."

"Just wait," she said. Her voice full of naughty promise. Facing him, her fingers went straight to the button of his jeans. The bulge behind the zipper made it a bit awkward to tug the thing down. This sweet, sexy guy wanted her and the knowledge did strange things to her heartbeat.

Zipper dispensed with, she smoothed her hands down his back, past the waistband of his jeans to cup his perfect muscular butt.

His eyes closed as she squeezed and pulled him into her. He sucked in a breath. She saw his hands fist at his sides. And she understood. Understood he was doing everything in his power not to yank her up against him, toss her on the bed and sink inside her.

Oh, that didn't sound half bad.

Miriam shoved those jeans down his thighs, dropping to her knees. She followed the path of his clothes with her mouth. Her tongue.

Her hands touched him everywhere, but not where she knew he desperately needed her contact. He growled as she purposefully missed his cock.

Then, when she sensed he'd suffered beyond what any healthy man could take, she wrapped her fingers around his penis and drew him to her mouth.

A more gentle woman might tease him. Draw her

tongue around his base. Stroke to the tip of him. Circle the head of his cock. Instead she drew him fully into her hot, wet mouth.

He groaned, his whole body shaking with the force of his need.

His hand sank into her hair, twining it gently around his fingers. The soft glide of him inside her mouth felt amazing. With an aching sound, he pulled himself from her mouth.

"On the bed," he said, reaching for a condom.

She glanced up, confused. "I wanted to give you pleasure this way."

He stopped what he was doing, his blue eyes almost black. "You will, but on that long drive here, all I could think of was feeling your hard nipples against my chest, the warmth of your breath against my neck, and those sexy little sounds you make as I drive into you."

She swallowed, her whole body shivering at his words. She wanted that, too. With a nod, Miriam stood and crawled up onto the bed. She draped herself across the mattress, parting her legs slightly. "What are you waiting for?"

Miriam watched as he ripped open the condom package with his teeth, then tugged the latex down his shaft. Seeing his hand on his cock, stroking himself, made her breath hitch. That hard piece of equipment would soon be in her, giving her pleasure.

He didn't even realize how sexy he looked preparing himself for her.

Task done, he joined her on the bed. He gripped her

hips and rolled onto his back, taking her with him. His fingers splayed at her hips, and she straddled him, her dark hair falling forward like a curtain.

"So this is how it's going to be," she said, breathless.

He nodded. "All I can think of now is you riding me, as I watch your breasts. You have amazing breasts. It's what kept me awake instead of exiting the highway and finding a motel to grab some sleep."

"Let me see if I can reward you." Miriam found the base of him, teased herself with the tip of his cock, then she decided to take pity on the poor man. Take pity on both of them. He'd driven all the way up to New York for her, after all.

She positioned him where he'd give her the most pleasure, then let gravity take over.

Jeremy sounded breathless as he fully seated himself inside her. "Miriam, you're amazing. Amazing."

She bit her lip. No, he was the amazing one. He didn't just do amazing things to her body, he made her feel amazing. As if she was more than a head of a multinational company. More than a reputation or money.

No, Jeremy made her feel like an object of desire. She would have slapped the face of any man who'd suggested she was such a thing, but Jeremy's objectification made her feel powerful. Safe enough to want to let her guard down a bit and be nothing but a sexual being in bed.

She lifted herself, then sank down on him again.

His eyes drifted shut, and she took selfish satisfaction in watching his face as he fought the passion. Then his eyes met hers, and there was that touch of something she'd spotted in him earlier. A vulnerability. "I can't hold out much longer. I've wanted you too long."

"Then don't hold out," she whispered and closed her eyes. She didn't want to see that unmasking of his emotions. She rubbed her breasts against his chest, just like he wanted, ground her body against his hardness.

He groaned again, then grabbed her hips, pushing himself into her over and over, until her muscles tensed around him. Until her climax overtook her, and she moaned with the force of the pleasure. Jeremy's orgasm hit him with force. His whole body tensed and shook. Feeling his reaction to her generated a second wave of pleasure through her body.

Afterwards she collapsed against him, her body covering him.

"As good as you remember?" she asked.

He nodded, his eyes still closed. "Better," he said, smiling in satisfaction.

Once she regained her breath, she slipped off him, took care of the condom, then snapped off the lights. She'd tug the covers up later. Right now she was still too hot.

Jeremy drew her close, resting her head against his chest. His steady heartbeat lulling her into sleep. "I'd hoped…I'd wanted to make love to you all night long, but after that drive, I'm sorry. I have to get some sleep."

She settled even more closely against him. "Jeremy, it's okay. Believe me, I got my money's worth. I came twice."

He gave her a tired smile.

"How long did it take you to drive?"

"Over twenty-four hours."

Miriam tried to picture the map in her mind, thinking of a logical place for him to stop. Indiana? Ohio? "Where'd you take your break?"

"I didn't. I drove straight through. Thought I might cash in at Philadelphia, but then…I just kept going."

Then, once he'd arrived, he'd had to check into a hotel. Find where she worked, and then she'd made him wait while she talked to her mother. The man must have been in agony, but he'd never let her know it.

She kissed his cheek. "Rest."

His heavy breathing was her only answer.

Her eyes began to drift shut, too. Might as well get some sleep now, because once Jeremy got his second wind, she suspected there wouldn't be much time for sleep. Nine or ten times.

She'd just about joined him in rest when her body jerked and her mind sent off the warning sequence. In fact, it had probably been sending out the signal and flares all along, only to be drowned out by lust and desire.

Jeremy had driven all the way from Oklahoma just to see her. He'd mentioned he'd thought of nothing else. He'd deprived himself in order to be with her sooner.

Had he read more into their weekend together? Was Jeremy feeling more for her than just passion? If she weren't careful, she'd shift into full-blown panic. And she hadn't panicked since, well, she couldn't think of a time when it had happened.

Actually, she could think of the last time she'd panicked. In a bed. In Oklahoma. With Jeremy.

9

IAN NUDGED HER HAND. "Ready to begin your observations? Check out this guy. He's going to try and approach that girl sitting at the bar."

The bar was more brightly lit than the rest of the club. Blue neon and lots and lots of bottles of alcohol backlit in front of a mirror. Dozens of high-backed chairs surrounded the serving area. Two women sat together talking over their glasses as a man made his way toward the pair.

Twenty-first-century man performing his mating ritual. This was exactly what Ian had wanted her to see. She settled back against the cushion of the couch to better monitor the situation.

Ian leaned closer to whisper into her ear so she could hear him above all the interesting noises in the bar. "She's going to blow him out of the water. He didn't do his legwork beforehand," his tone slightly disbelieving.

Ava narrowed her eyes. Prime research, and she'd worn an outfit with no place to hide a notebook. Thank goodness he'd suggested the purse. "What do you mean?"

"Watch."

The music thumped as she noted the predatory male approach the first woman and say something to her. The second female leaned over and spoke to the hunter. The man glanced down at the first woman he'd marked as his prey. She shook her head, and the man left. His shoulders stooped. His walk slower. Defeated.

"How did you know?" she asked, incredulous. And impressed. *She* was the one who was supposed to be the expert.

"First, look at the way he's dressed. He's a slob. You don't dress like that to meet a woman. Women notice crap like shoes. You dress nice for women. Clean, pressed clothes. Nothing in the grill. Comb your hair. It's a respect thing. This is war. You can't give a woman anything that will make her shoot you down before you open your mouth."

"This is fascinating stuff." *War?*

"Now, look at *their* clothes. They're in work clothes. They're here to unwind from a day at the office. Contrast that against your outfit." His gaze angled downward, stopped at her cleavage for a moment before working its way back toward her eyes. "You're dressed for having fun. *You're* the one men approach. Or at least men paying attention."

"How come you don't go over there and explain to that man why he failed?"

Ian shot her an incredulous look.

"In every culture, it's the responsibility of the more knowledgeable to teach the rest. That way their traditions and mores are passed on to future generations."

"In this culture, men don't inform other men how to score. Why give another man the advantage in battle?"

"Battle? War? Scoring? It's almost as if women are the enemy. There's a study in this. I know it." Ava opened her petite sequined purse and pulled out a small notebook.

"I can't believe you brought that."

"I'm always prepared for research." She squinted at the blank page. "Never mind. I can barely see." Ava replaced the pad in her purse and scanned the room.

"Not much research here anyway. Just your typical bar scene," he stated matter-of-factly.

She scanned the room. "I almost feel sorry for men. It's so dark in here. How can you even see the subtle cues and hints a woman drops?"

"Men adapt. And that's what the beer is for," he told her, lifting up his bottle as if making a toast. "False courage."

"So how did you learn?"

Ian shrugged. "I'm a reporter. My main job is to study people, look for weaknesses so I can get the information I want."

She'd have to keep that in mind. Was he hunting for her weakness even now? Ava shivered at the thought.

"But the main reason he failed earlier is because he didn't take into account the cockblocker."

Ava nearly choked on her appletini. "The what?"

He grinned at her. "Cockblockers are women whose main job is to block, or prevent, any man from infiltrating the group."

"And women are aware of these roles?"

Ian leaned closer as if he were going to impart a big secret. "Ordinarily women aren't around to hear it. I'm betraying man talk here."

Now *this* sounded very intriguing. "So are all men thwarted by the…cockblocker?"

"No, that's when you bring in your wingman. The wingman approaches the women, paying attention to the cockblocker, buying her a drink, chatting, whatever. Now here is how the scenario is played out. Once the wingman is in place, the other man approaches and acts surprised. 'I didn't know you'd be here.' Then the wingman introduces the two women and invites his friend to join them all." He shifted away from her, his smile very satisfied. "Pure gold I just shared with you."

"And you've tried this?" Ava asked, not bothering to hide the skepticism in her voice.

Ian shrugged. "Me? No, never. I prefer meeting women on my own."

"Care to share how? Because *this* I've got to hear." She leaned closer.

"Women don't go for a man who looks like a loser. He has to look like someone who's worth her time. Like I said, it's a respect thing. A man's got to have a game. A plan. You buy them a drink, never ask. You don't feed them a corny line. You say hello, smile, ask them if they're having a good time. Move on."

"Move on?"

"Women are expecting you to hang around. Show

them you're interested then go back to your table. Or play pool. Just something else. It makes the woman curious. Confuses her. It's a mystery thing. All women love a mystery."

Ava couldn't help it. She shook her head. "This is horrible. It's like battle plans, miscues and deliberate confusion. There's nothing sensual about it." She scowled. "Wait a minute. You're just messing with me like you did with the knights and the flower garland. I should have known. This sounds too unbelievable."

"Really? You'll never find out sitting here with me. There's only one way for you to truly understand North American mating customs—you have to experience them. You go up to the bar."

"And do what?"

"Wait."

"For what?"

"To be approached. Run a tab, I'll take care of that later." Then his expression hardened. "Don't worry, if anything weird happens, I'll step in," he assured her, his voice a little gruff.

Was he imagining other men trying to meet her and being jealous? Good.

Ava finished the rest of her drink, anticipation making her feel lighter. She adored participating in ceremonies and rituals from all over the world. That's when she felt in her element. Like now.

"Try to work in some of those subtle seduction techniques from your book."

"Excellent suggestion." She stood, smoothing down

her skirt. Ian's gaze followed the movement of her hands down her thighs.

That's right, buddy. That's the sensual game. I'll show you twenty-first-century male responding to the ancient techniques.

"And Ava," he said, his voice taking on that husky tone she was beginning to like so much. A tone that showed how much he liked looking at her body.

"Yes?" she said, flashing him a slow smile. She'd even throw in the head tilt.

"Don't drag out your notebook," he told her with a wink. A man secure in his environment and utterly confident.

Two can play it that way. She rounded her shoulders, her nipple pushing out the material of her blouse. "Don't worry. I'll know what to do."

That brash smile he'd flashed her faded. Besides, she'd forgotten her pen. Ava turned on her new high heels and, striding toward the bar, was careful to pick one of the bar stools that was not occupied on either side.

After ordering a white wine, she idly glanced up toward one of the many televisions throughout the club. This one appeared to be playing some type of athletic competition.

"If you like basketball, I can show you one of my trophies," a male voice suddenly said.

IAN WATCHED THE MAN approach Ava. He wasn't surprised. The guy had been checking her out since they'd walked in together.

What *did* surprise him was the twinge of unease he felt at seeing another man advance on her. He observed her sneak a subtle glance down at the man's shoes. Ian smiled. The little professor had obviously paid attention to some of his comments. Maybe he should make a few more about the idiots who'd try to pick her up. A couple stumbled in front of him, obscuring his vision of Ava for a moment. The music blared.

The two talked for a few minutes, actually, the man talked to Ava. Idiot. You didn't talk *at* a woman. You engaged them. Tried to make them laugh.

Ian relaxed. This clown would get nowhere. Then he saw a look of surprise pass across her face. Unpleasant surprise.

That unease he'd felt turned into a clenching of his stomach. What in the hell had the bastard said to her? Ian began to stand.

Then she nodded and they both looked around for… something. Finally, the guy leaned over and talked to the bartender, who then handed him a pen. Ian's breath came out in a disgusted hiss. He saw Ava recite something and the man wrote it down on a napkin.

Idiot. This guy didn't deserve her phone number if he didn't come prepared. And what had he said to her to manage to get her number? Maybe she didn't realize she was supposed to be selective when handing out her digits. Then he watched as the jerk kissed her temple and walked away.

That's right buddy, you just keep on moving. Ava was way out of his league.

The jerk was lucky he'd only kissed her temple.

Ava hopped off the bar stool, then lifted her wineglass and walked toward him. Ian liked the way the woman moved. Her hips rolled with the grace of someone not afraid of her body. She smiled, and his breath caught in his chest.

"I think I did okay," she said, her voice brimming with excitement. "Strange, awkward customs, but I could get the hang of it. What's traditional here? Thumbs-up? High five?"

"Ladies' room visit to scrub off the side of your face," he muttered under his breath.

Her brow furrowed in confusion. "And I see what you mean about corny opening lines."

"What did he say?" Ian asked, resentment making his words rush. If that man had said something crude to Ava he'd go over there right now and show him how a lady should be treated.

"Oh, something about showing me his trophies. It was mixed in with a sports reference so I didn't really understand all of it. But the gist of it was to try and be impressive and hint that all his *trophies* would follow suit."

Ian tasted something bitter in his mouth.

"He asked for my phone number."

"Yeah, I gathered that by all the fumbling around."

Her eyes grew sharper. "Okay, I can tell by your voice you're going to tell me he did something wrong. I checked out his shoes. They looked okay to me."

"He didn't have a pen. It looks unprepared. Incompetent. From the moment a woman notices a man, she's judging him. No woman wants to invest a lot of her time and energy into someone who will turn out to be a dud. You coming without a pen leads to questions like, 'what else will this guy forget?'"

Ava nodded. "Or, how incompetent will he be in bed?"

"Exactly."

She drew a deep breath. "Fine. I think I'm ready to return to the bar."

"What?" He hadn't expected he'd have to step back and watch her be approached by other men again. He opened his mouth to stop her, then—

Why did he care if some slob hit on her?

It wasn't as if he wanted her for himself.

He took a swig of beer, but it no longer tasted good. In fact, it was like lead in his stomach. He'd spent too much time alone and in too many dangerous situations not to trust his instincts and lie to himself now. *Yeah, I do want her for myself.*

Hell.

"Do you not think I should try again?" she asked, her fingers on his back.

Hmm? Oh, yeah. He'd just yelled "what" like a lunatic. Instead he offered another reply. Nodding, he said, "Sure, go back. Try some of those body language seduction techniques you talked about in the book." That should keep her busy. Ava didn't know how to talk to a man in a bar. Sure, he'd grant some of her ideas worked in a small way in a one-on-one situation over dinner, but here? Dim bar? Filled with drunk guys? No way. Subtle was not the answer.

"Universal flirting? Great idea." She finished off her wine, deposited her glass on the table and headed to the bar. Half a dozen male eyes following her progress. Laughing at him because it appeared he'd struck out.

None of these men knew what she looked like slathered in paint and wearing a loincloth. He did. His gut remembered. It tightened at the image.

That flashy top she wore was no match for that black miniskirt. Skirt or loincloth, he'd never get tired of watching Ava Simms's sweet ass.

Yeah, he was in trouble.

AVA SMILED AS SHE made her way back to the bar. He may not know it yet, but Ian didn't like the idea of her talking to other men. He wasn't the only observer of life. She was a trained scientist after all, and she knew when she spotted some pre-mate-guarding conduct.

He'd already pointed out the flaws in a potential rival. Classic male behavior. Anything else? Oh, yes, there was a gleam in his eye when he looked anywhere lower than her collarbone, and his hand gripped the bottle hard when she displayed mate-receptive behaviors. All excellent signs.

At the bar, this time she sat right next to a man sitting alone nursing something on the rocks.

Ava glanced toward Ian and noticed him glaring at the back of the man beside her. *Warning him off.* Another good sign. Her body warmed at Ian's behavior.

His brown-eyed gaze then met hers, and she sucked in her breath. There was heat and fire in that gaze.

Something tempting and full of sensual promise. Suddenly she began telling herself maybe they didn't have to stretch the sexual tension between them for the benefit of the book.

Maybe they could enjoy the sexual chemistry. As hot as the sensual energy zipping between them was, it couldn't help but make it onto the pages.

Her shoulders sagged, and she angled her body away from the man nearby. She didn't want to practice her flirting skills on anyone else but Ian. She certainly didn't want to make him jealous by leading on another man.

Ava only wanted Ian.

And to know he wanted her.

He'd teased her about some of the universal flirting techniques she'd postulated. But scientists had been studying them for decades, and she'd show him just how easily they worked. Right now. On him and no other.

After ordering another drink, she rounded her shoulders and positioned herself on the bar stool so her breasts were at their most perky, and her hip-to-waist ratio looked proportional. Subconsciously all men noticed that.

Then she tilted her head to the side, making her hair fall over her cheek. With a flourish, she tucked the strands behind her ear. Then slowly, she raised her eyes toward Ian. She knew he would be looking. She still felt his gaze on her. A sixth sense passed down from one generation to another.

Their gazes met again. The tiniest of smiles played

about her lips. Then Ava quickly looked away. She adjusted her hair again. Counted to three. Then glanced his way once more.

He'd been waiting for her. His shoulders tensed. His lips thinned.

Ava held his gaze with her own. Held it. Held it until it became just a tad uncomfortable. Counted to three, then dropped her eyes.

She took a sip of wine from the fresh glass the bartender had placed before her, the coolness of the white liquid not putting a dent in how hot she felt. She was supposed to be demonstrating to Ian the power of flirting. Not succumbing to his dark glances.

Ava crossed her legs and angled her body more in line with his—showing affinity. One more coy glance ought to do it. She lifted her eyes.

Slam.

He was standing, facing her. He'd been sitting the last time she'd looked in his direction.

Every part of this man was focused on her. His body was aligned to hers. His eyes, unwavering, never left her face. Anyone seeing his behavior toward her would see the primitive male claiming what was his.

Ava's nipples tightened. Her skin tingled. With a small nod, he moved toward her. His eyes never left hers as he wove his way between the tables and other patrons of the rapidly filling nightclub. The music pounded around them, the sound reminding her of a tribal drum beating a call. Her response to this man was primal and instinctive.

"Hello," he said as he approached. This man didn't need a corny line.

"Hi," she said, meeting his gaze.

"I'll give you my number, but only if you promise to stop flirting with me," he said, his tone lightening, that dimple in his cheek appearing once more.

10

"Is THAT WHAT I WAS DOING? Flirting with you?" she asked, chuckling.

This was fun.

She'd only spent a few semesters of college on campus. The rest of the time was spent on internships or practicums. When she had lived among her fellow college students, she'd been studying so much, she'd never had a chance to go for the club scene.

Ian signaled the bartender for another drink. "You know it is. And you still are."

She giggled then sighed inwardly. The female giggle was a flirting classic; one she particularly thought made her seem utterly vacuous. And here she was doing it. Damn instinct.

But men seemed to like it. Certainly Ian did because he began to finger the stem of her wineglass as he smiled down at her. Palming an object, particularly one that belongs to a love interest, definitely signaled his interest.

And also made her think of him touching her. Made her wonder what his hands would feel like on her body.

Would he be gentle and seductive? Or heated and filled with passion?

Might as well go for it. She flashed him another classic—the half smile. "You're right. See, I told you it worked. It got you over here. Now, you're supposed to impress me."

He raised an eyebrow.

"So, was that your best line?"

He shrugged. "Usually works."

Ava bet it did. She couldn't imagine it would be too hard for this man to have any woman he wanted. She planned to make him know *she* was the woman he needed at that moment. But disguised of course. Under the guise of "research."

"Now we're at the preening stage," she told him as the bartender landed a bottle of beer in front of Ian.

"Aren't I supposed to teach you about the local dating customs?"

"I learn best by doing. Why don't I demonstrate this stage, and you tell me if I'm doing anything wrong. I'll do stuff like toss my head, flip my hair, maybe dangle a strand around my finger." Ava demonstrated the moves as she spoke, thrilled that Ian's eyes clocked her every gesture.

Ava watched as he took a swallow of his beer. Who knew watching the way a man's throat moved as he drank was sexy? She'd never read this before. This definitely should be noted. "How'd I do?" she asked, as she reached for her purse. "The hair thing seems to be most effective worldwide."

He made some sort of noncommittal sound. What kind of confirmation, or nonconfirmation, was that? At some point, some less noisy place, she'd have to talk to him about clear, concise communication. It was imperative in research, and sometimes his signals were damned confusing.

"So do you plan to tell me what I'm supposed to do next?" he asked.

Her brow creased, and her voice lowered as if she were about to tell him a secret. "Actually, I think the man's next moves are somewhat tougher. You have to show how big and powerful you are. You'll be a little bit louder than I am. Your motions will be broader, demonstrating the strength of your hands and arms."

Ian shrugged, immediately drawing her attention to the impressiveness of his shoulders. Sturdy. Strong. In more primitive times, those flexing muscles would have proven he could protect their home from any fierce sharp-toothed prey that wanted to get her. In present-day Oklahoma, the demonstration of his brawn proved he could carry the heavy stuff out to her car.

The DJ played a new, louder song and it became more difficult for them to talk and be heard. She leaned toward Ian. "But here's the tricky part for you. Your body is saying to me, 'I'm powerful and tough, but I'd never, ever hurt you.' Strength coupled with tightly wielded gentleness is a heady combination."

He swallowed, his hands lowering to his sides. "You'll always be safe with me. Safe *from* me…now that's another story."

Her breath hitched at the promise she heard in his voice. She didn't need to be drawn into him. She was aiming for the other way around.

"I'll try to entice you further. I'll gaze longer into your eyes. Looking face-to-face with anyone demands a reaction. With a member of the opposite sex you find very attractive, it's exhilarating. Does this approach work here in this situation, too?" She held his gaze, her eyes narrowing slightly, her lips slowly parting.

He shifted, coming in closer to her. Right on cue. He probably hadn't even realized it, but he was testing the boundaries of her personal space. She felt the heat of his body now. Saw the lights from the dance floor reflecting in his eyes.

She twisted on the bar stool, facing him. He followed suit. They'd successfully passed the preening look-at-me stage and were now in full-body synchronization. Her stomach muscles tightened.

Now on to real intimacy. "One thing that's almost universal in flirting is a woman exposing her neck." Ava tilted her head, allowing her hair to slide over her shoulder and down her back. "Early research suggested this was a sign of submission."

His eyes widened.

She gently ran her fingers down her neck, traced the line of her collarbone. Her movements were supposed to draw Ian's thoughts to following that same path. With his fingers. His mouth. But it also got her imagination leaping in that direction.

Ava cleared her throat. "But I don't think it has

anything to do with submission. I think it's about invitation. There's something about the gentle lines of a woman's neck that draws a man's eye. It's an erogenous zone. I think presenting my neck says to a man, 'This is a place where you can make me feel good.' It's a challenge." Their gazes clashed once more. "Can you make me feel good, Ian?"

Her question was supposed to tantalize him, but teased her with images of him giving her pleasure. With his mouth. With his hands. However he wanted to make her feel good.

"Yes," he replied. His voice was filled with a charged promise. He leaned even closer.

She felt even more of his heat.

"Now I pull back," she told him as she scooted away from him on her bar stool. Ava turned, positioning her chest toward the bar once more, even though she'd liked exactly where she'd been.

Confusion filled his eyes. "Why?"

Ava shrugged. This was the hardest to explain. Even to herself it felt strange. "Ancient female tests. I call it the Promise Withdrawal Cycle. It's the promise for more intimacy quickly followed by withdrawal."

Ian's body stiffened. "I know exactly what you're talking about. Women do that all the time. Why?"

"It's a time-honed combination of playing hard to get and testing your staying power. To see if you'll stick around. Of course that was a lot more important when women stayed by the fire in the cave and couldn't go out to hunt the mammoth themselves. A typical man will have two reactions. He's either annoyed or his interest is piqued ever further. As a woman I note your expressions and your body language in less than a second. If you get frustrated, start looking around the room, I know you don't have what it takes."

"But if I lean closer, try harder…" His voice trailed off, but he followed up his words with actions. Ian lowered his head, his lips moved just above her ear. "Say something like 'Ava, I would never hurt you. I would only ever want to make you feel good.'"

His voice was a sensual caress, his words a sexy reminder of his tempered strength. She felt his breath on her skin. This man got what she was saying. A tiny thrill ran down her back. Her nerve endings reared up and she grew invigoratingly aware of his scent, the expression in his eyes and the subtle movements of his hands.

"I'll invite physical contact. Most people think men are the true aggressors, but it's really women who initiate that first touch. A mature man waits for the invitation, knows how to bide his time for the payoff. I might do something like reach over and pull off an imaginary thread from your shirt."

Ava stretched her arm, her fingers lightly brushing his shoulders. She felt the muscles tense below her fingertips. She was affecting him, and that felt very, very good.

"Now that I have your full attention, I'll take my drink, play with the straw, bring it to my mouth."

His eyes shifted to her lips and he exhaled a breath.

Then back again to her eyes.

His pupils were more dilated.

"I want you to think about my mouth," she explained as she sipped her wine. The waiter had looked at her as if she was crazy when she'd asked for the straw, but she knew what she was doing.

He ran a finger along the collar of his shirt. "I never knew how hot this flirting research could be."

Her gaze was drawn to the skin below his ear. Would he be sensitive there, like her? His mouth thinned, as if he guessed her thoughts. Good. He was becoming more in tune with her. Of course it wasn't as if she were trying to hide that she was thinking about sex. Sex with him.

"Over time, women developed a set of skills to test men in a very short period of time. It's a back and forth. I make a move, you make a move. It's actually quite sophisticated. If it's working, you'll know we'll be on the same page while in bed."

His gaze heated. "You're making me a believer."

"There's only one other sure way a woman can verify she'll be compatible with a man before sex."

His brows lifted. "I can't wait to hear it."

She eyed the couples out on the dance floor. Some moving with grace, others encompassing the more sensual movements. "We dance."

"I'll order you another drink." Ian signaled for the bartender.

Ava frowned. "Why?"

"Modern dating tip. Men become better dancers as women drink more."

Ava laughed. Not exactly the response from him that she'd been looking for—she'd been hoping he'd nearly yank her onto the dance floor so he could finally have her in his arms. But funny always worked in a man. "How many more drinks before you're out under those flashing lights with me?"

"Oh, I'd say a lot."

The bartender delivered another one of those green drinks and a shot of something for him. She sipped from her martini glass, loving the tart sweetness of it. Silence. It could be uncomfortable and awkward. But right now, it just stretched the anticipation, the wonder of what would happen next.

The tempo of the music changed, from hard drumbeats to soft lilting guitar. The lights dimmed, and she imagined gliding around on the dance floor, his strong arms around her.

Something like determination molded his features. He downed his drink in a swallow, met her eyes then offered his hand.

With a half smile, she replaced her martini glass on the bar and stood. She lifted her fingers to his, and his hand engulfed hers in warmth.

He found a secluded spot on the dance floor where the lights were dimmer and drew her into his arms. Close, so she felt the heat of him, couldn't miss the sexy scent of him. But not so close she felt intimidated by his size. Somewhere along the way, Ian Cole had picked up how to treat a woman.

They moved to the music slowly. "You're a good dancer." She looked at him with surprise after his dancing protests from a few moments ago.

Even in the low light, she could see the weird face he'd made at her compliment. "My father made sure my sister and I had dance lessons."

"Actually, that's a good thing. I'll give you a tip. A woman can tell a lot by how a man handles himself while dancing. His confidence. How comfortable he feels with his own body. How he moves."

"And how are my moves?" he asked as his fingers caressed the small of her back.

The man gave her shivers.

"Not bad. But it's more than just your moves a woman is examining. You show me something about yourself as a man by not allowing other dancers to bump into me or take up our dancing space. A woman's mind begins to imagine. Is he adventurous with his—"

"I'll give you a tip." His thumb traced her bottom lip and her words died. In fact, just what had she been going to say?

He drew her closer into the heat of his body. His gaze never left hers.

"Just dance with me," he said. "No more talking about flirting. What we should be doing. I want only this."

Ava closed her eyes when his fingers sank into her hair, the caress against her scalp. He drew her head to his shoulder, the softness of his shirt smooth under her cheek.

He was right. With his strong arms surrounding her, the brush of his thighs against her as they moved, the last thing she wanted to do was discuss the social importance of dancing. She wanted to experience the dance. And that was the first time she'd ever truly wanted to be a participant rather than a cultural observer.

The song ended, the tempo of the music quickened, and Ian led her off the dance floor, their fingers twined together. He wore the confident look of a man who had a woman exactly where he wanted her. Lesson number two for her. She finally understood the battle between the genders she'd observed earlier, and which Ian mentioned. The subtle love play that kept one partner as the lead.

She'd had the lead until the dance. She wanted it back. "Ian, I didn't tell you the surefire way a woman secures a man's attention."

"One more might kill me," he said, that sexy smile showing her he wasn't really worried.

She drew her fingertips down his jaw, and his smile faded. "Make him know you're a bad idea. Men always want what they shouldn't have."

He arched a brow. "Oh, yeah, like how?"

"By telling you the truth." Ava tucked a strand of hair behind her ear, licked her lips and shyly met his gaze. Then she held it, angling her body toward him. All at once the shy seductress and bold temptress. "This isn't a good idea. It might ruin everything. Our work," she said, her voice almost a whisper.

Ian leaned closer. His expression determined to know her meaning. "What might ruin everything?"

"Getting involved. Having sex."

Ian swallowed. She almost felt sorry for him. After all, she'd brought out all the big weapons a woman possessed. She knew how to use them.

Ava wanted to make him burn. She wanted him to want her so badly he thought of nothing else.

She wanted to feel it, too.

He flashed her a sexy, crooked smile. Ahh, men must have that move ingrained in their DNA. Crooked smiles made a woman think mischievous. And mischievous suggested all kinds of naughty and delightful things between the sheets.

"Let's get out of here," he ordered, his voice deep and seductive.

"I still have my drink," she told him, not the least bit thirsty.

His eyes grew alarmed. "Leave it. I'll buy you another. That's a modern dating tip. Never leave your drink unattended then consume more."

"It seems such a waste."

"I'll show you what's going to waste." Ian lowered his head, his lips lightly brushing hers. "Still thirsty?" he asked against her mouth, his breath a warm caress against her cheek.

She shook her head.

"Good." He reached for her hand again, leading her through the couples and weaving between the tables until they were outside.

The cold chill of the winter air nipped at her skin, but she didn't feel a thing. That light teasing kiss Ian had given her had heated her from the inside, and she was ready for more.

The Bricktown sidewalks teemed with activity. The bright streetlights illuminated their path as they made their way amongst the other late-night revelers. The street vendors had gone, replaced by rickshaws. A police officer patrolling on his bicycle rode past as they walked toward her building.

Any other night she'd want to take it slow. Enjoy the ambiance and people watch. But this wasn't any ordinary night. Tonight Ian held her by the hand, and she was ready for him to demonstrate the promises his body had made to her on the dance floor.

Everything about him suggested he'd be an unselfish lover. And could there be anything sexier than a man who cared about his woman's pleasure?

In what felt like way too long a walk, they approached her apartment. In the shadows he pulled her into his arms. Ava stretched, looping her arms around his neck, tangling her fingers in his hair. Their gazes locked briefly in the moonlight.

"You want me to tell you how I kiss a woman, Ava?"

No. She wanted him to show her. Right now.

"I touch her face. Cup her cheek. Then I let my hands slide down her shoulders. Her arms. Just a gentle glide. Make her feel comfortable. Let her know I'd never do anything she doesn't want me to do to her body."

His actions, followed only seconds after his words, was utter seduction, drawing out her anticipation, making her ache to feel what he described.

"I stop at her waist. That safe spot between your hips and your breasts is pure temptation. I can move my hands up or down and be in heaven."

When had he stopped talking in the abstract? Now

he was talking only about her. How parts of her were heaven to him. Some of those parts started to get really excited about the prospect.

"What shall it be?" he asked, his gaze lowering to her lips for a moment before returning to her eyes.

He didn't wait for her response. His fingers cupped her hips and he drew her closer. The tips of her breasts brushed his chest, her nipples hardening at the contact. Her eyes drifted shut for a moment at the exquisiteness of the sensation. As a scientist, she'd studied gender response, researched the origins of customs related to sex and observed the intricate human behaviors that led to it, but experiencing her own response to Ian was intense.

His head descended, but instead of finding her lips, the firm softness of his mouth drifted along her neck. Tingles shot out to everywhere in her body.

"Remember you asked if I were up for the challenge? Could I give you pleasure here?" His breath sent a shiver down her sensitive skin.

His lips slid a slow path down her neck. Across the exposed area of her collarbone. She sucked in a breath when he followed with his tongue.

Yes. Ian Cole was definitely up for the challenge.

His hands caressed her through her shirt, running up and down her back. Shivers of sensation crisscrossed her spine.

"A less patient man might go straight for your mouth. A hard, hungry kiss to show you how hard and hungry I am. But I won't do that."

"You won't?" she asked, unable to mask her disappointment.

"No, a woman like you appreciates a man willing to take risks, not give you what you expect."

Ian kissed both of her closed eyes. The tip of her nose. Each time she sensed his lips getting closer to hers, she raised her mouth, tried to finally feel his lips.

When he began kissing her forehead she'd had enough. Ava opened her eyes to see Ian smiling at her. Gentle, as though he knew he'd been driving her crazy, but his eyes were dark, so she understood he had been waiting, just like her.

"Kiss me, Ian."

"Just waiting for the invitation." He lowered his head and his lips lightly touched hers. Brushed hers for a moment. Then his lips firmed and he kissed her. Passion ignited between them. Burned. Ian kissed her as if he'd rather kiss her than breathe.

Her fingers twined in the hair at his nape. Her heart pounded. The blood rushed in her ears. Ava pressed her body close.

Ian broke off the kiss. The heaviness of their breathing filled the night air. She moaned in disappointment.

"Ava, I haven't shared with you the last tip," he said.

Her lids lifted and she looked into his eyes, clearing away the confusion his kiss caused. "What?"

He dropped his arms. "Always leave them wanting more." He leaned in and kissed her forehead. "Good night," he whispered.

After making sure she entered her building safely,

Ian turned swiftly and headed back down the sidewalk in the direction of his hotel.

Her whole body ached with sexual frustration.

Irritation.

Aggravation made her movements jerky as she let herself into her apartment.

Annoyed—yes. Disappointed—for sure. But secretly impressed by his ability to turn the tables on her—yes, she was that, too. "Well played, Mr. Cole. Well played."

_11_

Ava Simms was one hell of an adrenaline rush. Still, kissing her was not one of Ian's best moves.

Actually, it had been a great move.

But walking away before he suggested something stupid like continuing their research up in her bedroom was his best move of the night.

Ava possessed the kind of lips that invited a man's eyes. A call to investigate. Luckily, that fit right in with his chosen profession of journalist. He could easily spend the next few weeks working on her manuscript all the while exploring the woman. Studying the way her body matched perfectly to his. Or discovering new ways to have her make those sexy little sounds she'd made when their kiss deepened. Her soft moans fired something in his blood.

He could better use his time examining why she made him uneasy. As a reporter, Ian trusted his instincts when they warned him something wasn't exactly as it appeared. And Ava Simms was definitely not the almost-mild-mannered anthropology professor she seemed.

Somehow he knew she'd been expecting him to make a move on her, had been building every moment they had together to that point. It was as if she had something to prove about the validity of her theories and ideas, and he was the guinea pig.

Normally, if a smart, desirable and beautiful woman wanted to test her sexual ideas on his body, who was he to get in the way of science?

But he didn't usually *work* with smart, desirable women. Mostly it was a bunch of smelly angry guys alongside him in the field, if he worked with anyone at all. Quite frankly, he didn't have the skill set for this scenario.

Which was maybe what his sister liked about sending him here to Oklahoma. Miriam, she had a sadistic streak in her where he was concerned. Probably payback for the time he gave all her Barbies buzz cuts before he'd allow them to play with his G.I. Joe. Could be the fact her face was plastered across Do Not Allow into the Country posters in at least one South American country because of him. Or maybe it was for allowing her to do all the heavy lifting as far as their mother was concerned. Probably all three.

His sister wouldn't like the idea of him getting involved with Ava. That, of course, would have been incentive in itself, but he'd long since grown up and quit trying to shock Miriam. She was the only person in this world whom he knew who actually gave a crap about him, and he loved her for it.

Loved her so much that he'd be up at six o'clock in

the morning in Oklahoma completing a full edit on a sex book that should be titillating but wasn't. That was until he pictured the author.

Which brought him back full circle to Ava.

Damn. His body reacted just to the thought of her. Knowing she was trying out all her theories and techniques on him didn't prevent them from working on him. Since he'd met her, he'd been surrounded by images of sex. Not to mention the scents that also made him think only of sex. And now he had to read about it. And damn if that infuriating aroma of cinnamon didn't turn him on.

Maybe she did have something with that flower garland story. He had to admit he'd much rather twist a bunch of carnations together than tell her just how much work her *Recipe for Sex* needed. That quick read-through he'd given it on the plane hadn't revealed all the problems.

He should probably try to figure out why he didn't want to hurt her feelings. This was work. It wasn't personal. He'd never been one not to tell it to someone straight. His career was based on just the facts.

Yeah, he should probably scrutinize those feelings, but he wouldn't. He preferred to keep his emotions in the shallow end of the pool. A lesson learned early, and one that had never failed him.

THREE HUNDRED AND twenty-seven manuscript pages.

Three hundred and twenty-seven manuscript pages she'd written in a frenzy of anguish and drive. Nineteen-hour days, restless nights and little food had been Ava's life until she had finally typed *The End*. She'd poured her heart, as well as every other body part she possessed, into *Recipe for Sex*.

Three hundred and twenty-seven pages that were now covered from top to bottom, left to right in red ink. Some of her writing had apparently been so bad he'd had to make notations on the back. With drawings. This didn't include the sticky notes. Or the seven pages of notes he'd scribbled on a yellow legal pad.

She could almost feel his irritation in the large red X's that annihilated every paragraph in chapter three. The force from his pen had left an impression three pages down.

"No, no. That's all wrong," Ian told her for about the billionth time as he turned a page. She'd almost stopped paying attention.

He'd showed up at her apartment this morning with bagels, coffee and a determination to cross out months of her hard work with that lethal red pen of his. He'd looked innocent enough, wearing jeans and an Oklahoma Sooners T-shirt he must have bought since his arrival. Innocent for someone who was about to rip her heart out with his critique. Although *critique* was too nice a word because he'd found nothing positive.

His eyes flared a bit when she opened the door to him wearing the ceremonial dress of the Hidali.

"At least it's more than paint," he mumbled as he slid past her into her apartment. But she couldn't tell if he was happy about that or disappointed.

But her attire wasn't much more than paint as the Hidali hailed from Africa and the clothing took into account the heat, and the beauty of the flora that lent to the dyes. The colorful material was free-flowing and quite sheer.

"There's an elaborate meal that goes with this costume. I thought we could try it at lunchtime. I've already prepared the food. One of the dishes has some real aphrodisiacal properties."

Ian raised his hand. "Please. Let me at least fortify myself with coffee before you start talking about phallic symbols and food that's supposed to make any normal man hard while you're half-naked."

He made decidedly for her kitchen.

There was no mention of the kiss the night before.

Not that she'd expected it. Today's agenda was apparently going to be all about work. Evidently, Mr. Cole took to heart that not-mixing-business-with-pleasure axiom, because ten minutes later they were going over the manuscript together page by page. That red pen was finding things it had missed with Ian's first read through.

Ava gasped when he proceeded to X out one of her favorite sections.

"This whole section should go. It's dry and boring."

She shook her head. "It is not. Certainly the Bogani people whose culture you just obliterated from the page didn't think so."

Ian picked up the page. "'In ancient times, as now, in isolated communities in the mountainous region of Bogan, the men eligible to leave their mothers and fathers were gathered together in the village square where everyone dropped their heads and snored because these paragraphs would put anyone to sleep, even a boy about to lose his virginity.'"

She took a deep breath. "Maybe it's a tad uninspired."

He looked up from the page. "Uninspired? Ava, when we're talking about sex, the last thing it should ever be is uninspired."

Ava dropped her gaze. She'd acknowledge that he had a point about her writing, but not that the section needed to go. She'd sat silent for too long, and it was time for Ian to do a little compromising. "Okay, let's rewrite that portion."

Ian raised a brow. "We're not targeting virgins or even near-virgins with this book."

"Come on, Ian. You mean somewhere along the line, you wouldn't have wanted some older, experienced woman to show you the ropes in bed?"

"Well, it's been a long time since I was inexp—"

Ava rolled her eyes. "Oh, spare me that. Even when you know your way around the bedroom, when you're with a new person there are still nerves involved. Premature ej—"

"Not an issue," he said quickly.

"You mean, you've never had your skyrocket in flight long before hers?"

He swallowed. His skin reddened a bit. "My technique might not have been always airtight when I first started, but now…"

"My point exactly. Readers with a wide range of experiences will be reading this book." She refrained from rolling her eyes again. Male pride on prowess in the bedroom also seemed to be pretty universal. Here it seemed to manifest itself by preferring to fumble around in the dark rather than acknowledge suggestions.

"I know you said the other day that men don't give other men tips to score, but surely a man would take advice from a woman."

Ian crossed his arms across his chest, his expression confident. Overconfident. "Okay, shoot me a pointer."

She was up for the challenge. "Hmm. The first thing a Bogani woman shows the young lover is how to pleasure a woman using only his fingers."

"Of course she does." He made a scoffing sound, but his eyes narrowed in interest.

"A woman can be pretty forgiving of three-pumps-and-he's-done if she's already had at least one orgasm. Something to keep in mind if a man wants to be invited back to the bedroom for a repeat performance."

That overconfident expression he'd worn slipped a little. "Maybe you do have a point about this section."

Oh, yeah, she'd show him. Reaching for her remote, she turned on her stereo and selected music from the Bogani region. Her apartment was soon filled with the sounds of drums. Primal. Like the steady rhythm of a heartbeat.

Then she reached and took that hateful red pen from his fingers and dropped it to the floor. "The Bogani are a close-knit, family-oriented culture."

He mouthed the word *boring*. So she reached for the thick stack of pages comprising her printed manuscript. "Obviously you can improve upon my writing, but you need to actually experience this to truly understand what I'm trying to convey."

He cocked his head. A study in disbelief.

"I wouldn't have understood a singles bar until I experienced it."

Ian let her tug the papers from his hand easily. "I've already crossed this section out."

"I'm putting it right back in. The way the Bogani men learn to pleasure a woman will not only be helpful to less experienced men who might be reading the book, but could also be a fun role play. Dual purpose."

"Role play?" he asked. "Now that's some inspiration." His eyes let her know he was more than curious about her next move.

That next move led to her couch.

"You won't need your laptop, either," she told him as she reached for his hand and drew him away from the kitchen table he'd commandeered for the butchering of her masterpiece.

"The Bogani people frown on couples separating, and believe pleasure in the marriage bed makes for a happy union," Ava told him as she tugged him into her front room.

"Sometimes not even *that* can save a marriage."

Mr. Cynicism was back. Good. She liked demonstrating her techniques to him best. Made it all the sweeter when her point was successfully proven. "True, but it's never a reason for a breakup. That's where the widows come in. Some say they make the bed play work. Plus they're going to save this section from your red pen. And this time, it won't be dull."

"Been giving this some thought?"

"Actually it just came to me. Sit."

Ian made himself comfortable against the cushions of her couch while she kicked off her sandals.

"When a man has proven he can support himself and leave his parents, he's also free to be chosen by one of the widows to show him how to pleasure a woman," she sat beside him on the couch, his jeans-clad thigh brushing along her bare skin.

"She'd have to choose the man she'd tutor carefully, for he'd pay a yearly tribute to her until his death. It's actually a nice little social system. It ensures that women without protectors are provided for, while potentially removing one of the major barriers to marital happiness."

"Are there jealousies?"

Ava shook her head. "No. Once he marries, he and the widow don't see one another again. If the widow has done her job well, the wife has nothing but praise for her. Bogani place high importance on monogamy. Although the widow walks a fine line. She knows she's there as a teacher, and strives to make the process without intimacy."

"How does she do that?" he asked.

"By never making eye contact. By never talking about anything other than how to pleasure his future wife. Every touch, every caress, every new sensation is all encased in the future."

Ava deliberately lowered her gaze. Now she'd show him how lovers could role-play the Bogani teaching times.

"Boys and girls were usually separated from one another, learning the skills needed to keep their tribe thriving, so when they eventually make it back together, there's a lot of curiosity and shyness. So the first thing the widow teacher would do would be to make him feel comfortable with a woman's body. Receiving her touch and giving his. That first meeting he'd usually only stroke her."

Without looking up, she lifted his hands to the bare skin of her shoulder. He was warm and solid, and even with the barest of touches, not pulling off the inexperienced young man illusion very well.

"She'd instruct him how to run his fingers gently along her exposed skin. Softly caressing all the erogenous zones on a woman. Her neck. Her ears. How to sink his fingers into her hair, stroke her scalp. A lot of this can be missed in today's rushed lovemaking."

Ian followed her instructions perfectly. Deliciously. Her skin grew warm under his fingertips, achy for more of his touch. With shaky knees, Ava stood, still not meeting his eyes.

"Then she'd lead him to the small of her back. With even the lightest pressure there, the muscles loosen and it feels so good."

She sucked in a breath when Ian's fingers eased the tension that had gathered in that spot after seeing her book covered in red.

"The more relaxed a woman is, the easier her blood

is flowing through her veins, the quicker it is for her to reach her peak."

"Are you feeling relaxed, Ava?"

Like jelly.

Ava wanted to raise her gaze. To see into his eyes. To gauge his expression, and see if it matched the husky aroused sound of his voice. But she didn't. That's what made this experience so unique, so intense and yet slightly detached. Western cultures placed a lot of emphasis on meeting another's eyes. By not, the whole dynamic between two people completely changes.

Like now.

"He could slide his hands down. The skin behind the knee is very sensitive. Or she may suggest he find her inner elbow with his mouth."

Ian did both. The warmth of his tongue was a purely erotic sensation against her skin. Detached? Who was she kidding? She felt fully engaged.

"When does he kiss her?" he asked, his voice rough and low and sexy as hell. Ian had even added a move of his own, gently blowing against the bare skin of her stomach, the warmth making her tingle.

"He doesn't," she said, her voice sounding close to a moan. He tugged her closer toward him and his tongue began to wind a lazy path along her collarbone and slowly moved to below her ear.

Ava was losing the upper hand. She needed to stay focused. *Fall back on research.*

"You know there are many cultures that never kiss, the Inuit in Alaska being the most well-known. Across the world from the Americas, the Pacific areas and Africa, we find many people that never touched lip to lip. Although researchers documented the kiss first in India, dating it as far back as 1500 BCE."

His hands curved around her hips and drew her still nearer to the heat of his body. She lost her balance and landed in his lap. Startled, she finally met his eyes. Dark brown and full of intense heat and hunger. Intimate.

"Good thing that no-kissing rule doesn't extend to my culture." Then Ian lowered his head, his lips on hers. Heaven. His lips were firm and something elemental exploded inside her.

She wanted more, but Ian broke off the kiss. He smoothed the sweep of her hair over her shoulder and kissed her neck. Licking that place below her ear.

"This is not what we're supposed to be doing here. The Bogani women are always in control and would never allow the man to take over like this."

"Oh, yeah?" His nipped her earlobe. "Tell me what else we're not supposed to be doing."

Her fingers traveled up his to grasp the muscles of his shoulder. Then she sank her fingers into the hair at his neck. She'd loved the feeling of his hand stroking her scalp. Loved hearing his breath quicken when she did the same.

"I shouldn't be on your lap like this." His thighs hardened beneath her.

"Maybe you shouldn't press your breasts against my chest. I'd hate that."

Her nipples drew taut, the sheer fabric not hiding her

body's response to his words. Ava flattened herself against him, and he groaned.

"A Bogani widow would spend a whole day teaching a man how to touch a woman's breasts. To caress and stroke and finally lick."

"I don't know if I could last a whole day," he said next to her throat. His hand moved to cup her breast, his thumb finding and circling her nipple.

She cried out at the hot pleasure of his touch. "I have faith in you."

"Glad someone does," he said as his lips claimed hers once more.

This was no playful, teasing kiss. Ian almost growled when she touched her tongue to his. She hadn't expected the near-instant sexual connection she'd have with Ian to be so strong. So primal.

But sometimes that's what you got, and it was a rare, precious thing, so why not go for it? His fingers dipped for the ties holding the Hidali costume in place. "I had about a million reasons in my mind why we shouldn't have sex." His whispered words sent a thrill through her veins.

"Me, too."

His gaze sharpened. "You did? You've been thinking about having sex with me, but discounted it?"

She blinked up at him, missing the heat that was now fading in his eyes. "Sure. I want you. DNA programming. I found you attractive the moment you spoke."

His eyes narrowed. "So, it's just biology? Has nothing to do with me…personally."

"That's right. Sex is a normal, natural part of life. If I've observed anything since I've been back, it's that people seem to make such a big deal about doing the deed," she said with a shrug.

He didn't respond for a moment, as if he were considering her words carefully. "Well, if it's just sex, a totally biological function, then let's do it."

"Do what?"

A dark flame lit in his brown eyes. "Let's have sex. Right here. We don't even have to break out the paints. Just you, me and that rumble-drum music."

She tightened her arms around him. "Sure."

Ian made a strange sound in the back of his throat. "I know you've been away for a while, and so have I for that matter, but usually women aren't so...so..."

"So what?"

"So okay with just being biological."

"What do you mean?"

He gently pushed her out of his lap and stood. "We're missing the game playing, the pretending. Me trying to ramp up the action. You countering with a token denial."

"And that's what you want?"

He began to pace. "No, but it's what I'm used to."

"Ian, look. I don't know what to say. Obviously my experience level with dating normal people isn't very high, but it seems to me most problems between a man and woman could be cleared up with one good sit-down conversation."

He stopped his pacing and faced her. "You're right."

"I don't want to give you a token denial, but the truth

of the matter is I didn't really act on my attraction to you because this…this tension between us, this heat, I think it will translate on the page of the book. We could get…biological now. I have these great oils I'd love to try—they're all the way from Bolivia. Or we could work on the book and wait."

Strange how at that precise moment the intensity of the drum music lessoned. Near silence descended upon them as she waited for his decision.

Ian sank against the cushions of her couch. His breath came out in sharp frustrated exhalations. Then his gaze cut to hers.

"You have a natural instinct for picking customs that would be interesting and instructional to today's lovers. But you're terrible at choosing chapter titles and you bog down the flow with too much history."

"I won't be left out of the writing."

"I don't plan to cut you out. Before, when you told me of the Bogani women, that was exciting. That was different and that's what people would want to read about. When you tell me about these people, their beliefs, you make them come alive. Seem like living, breathing people that anyone can relate to, can swap lives with, even for just an evening. That's what this book needs."

She glanced down at the manuscript pages covered with his red scribbles. "Obviously I'm not very good at putting my thoughts on paper."

"That's where I come in. I'm going to interview you. Every ceremony, every food, every dance you'll share with me. Together we'll get this book written."

She nodded, liking the idea. "I think that could really work."

Ian stood, reaching for all the papers of her manuscript and stuffing them into the empty space in his laptop bag. "We won't be needing these. We'll start from scratch tomorrow, when we're fresh."

Ava followed him to the door. She leaned against the wall after he left, picking at a bead on her bodice.

Ian had chosen the book over making love to her.

She would ignore that let-down feeling.

12

AVA GREETED HIM wearing jeans and a light gray hoodie. She'd pulled her hair back in a ponytail, and Ian realized he liked this casual Ava. Hell, he just liked looking at the woman.

Today they'd be working on the chapter on scents. With that damn cinnamon, Ava had made him a believer that a man did respond on an elemental level. At least in a small way. But he wouldn't be lying if he said he'd been looking forward to this day of writing as a relief from the sexual tension brewing between them. Just how out of his mind would he get smelling from a few vials?

She smiled when she spotted his laptop case. "Don't you think we should experience this together before writing about it?"

"I like to be prepared."

"I'll remember that about you," she said with a wink.

She was doing it again. Turning his innocent comments into something that sounded like a double entendre. As if he was prepared for sex with a condom all at the ready. Or maybe that was in his own mind. She spent most of her life out of the country—did she even know what she seemed to be implying? He was going crazy.

"I've set everything up in the front room."

He'd expected vials and incense and containers of oil. Cotton swabs to capture the scents. What he hadn't prepared for was the scene she'd set up. Ava had been very industrious, pushing back the couches and making a pallet on the floor with colorful blankets, no doubt weaved on the bare thighs of women preparing for sex or some such story designed to push him over the edge.

Two large pillows, presumably where he was supposed to sit, were surrounded by lit candles.

Holy hell.

She reached for his hand. "Take off your shoes and come with me," her voice an invitation to be wicked.

Her soft fingers tightened around his after he'd kicked off his shoes, and she led him to the pillows, reclining on the one facing him.

"These candles are unscented so they won't mask the smells we're trying to explore, but set a nice mood. Rather than just list the fragrances that the opposite sex finds attractive, I thought it would be far more interesting to dab the oils on our bodies."

Of course she'd have that idea. Ava Simms had lots of great ideas on how to torture him sexually.

"Are we talking pheromones?"

She shook her head. "As subconscious sex attractants, nothing can beat them, but it's thought that only eighty percent of humans have the organ to even sense them. Some researchers think even less can detect pheromones due to disuse. Those odds are terrible. Why leave something like that to chance?"

He was beginning to think Ava didn't leave much to chance. Him, he'd take a little mystery.

"So humans found a way to maximize the senses we do have." Ava reached for a lighter and lit a thin stick. "Patchouli awakens sexuality, and comes from the tropical areas in Asia. Incense is the easiest way to find it."

He watched as Ava delicately blew out the flame on the stick and waved a cloud of smoke around them. Despite his late night, he was now wide awake.

She'd closed her eyes and took a deep breath. His body hardened as he watched her enjoy the smell surrounding them. This woman took pleasure in so many things.

She opened her eyes and smiled. "It's kind of sweet and earthy," she said as she placed the stick on an ornately carved holder. "Patchouli is thought to alleviate anxiety, so it might be a good scent for first-time lovers."

She kept bringing up the topic of first-time lovers, which always brought the prospect of the two of them being first-time lovers.

Ava reached for a vial beside her. "This is ylang-ylang. That means wilderness, and is used as a true aphrodisiac in the South Pacific." She rubbed a small drop of it on the crease of her elbow.

"Every aroma takes on a whole different personality when on the skin. It mixes with our own natural scents and musks and creates something totally unique." She shifted toward him. "Smell."

He'd kissed this woman. Stroked her skin, cupped

her breast, but there was something about lowering his head to breathe in the scent of her that was wholly intimate and erotic.

Ian wasn't up on his scents. He couldn't tell you the difference between jasmine and lavender, but he could say that what Ava rubbed on her skin made him think of nothing but raw lovemaking.

A slow smile curved her full lips. "Powerful, isn't it? Ylang-ylang boosts the attraction between a man and a woman. Enhances energy and open-mindedness."

His imagination sure wasn't having any trouble. Right now his mind was coming up with all kinds of energetic scenarios from pushing Ava back against that pillow to—

"Vanilla is particularly attractive to women." She reached for a brown bottle. "This is pure vanilla extract that you can find in any grocery store. Not good to taste, but if you were to put some on your neck, I would keep getting closer and closer to you as the evening progressed."

And here he'd been wasting all this money on expensive colognes.

"So do you think this will work for the book?"

All Ian could do was nod.

MIRIAM WATCHED AS JEREMY stretched in her bed, the sheets twisting around his flat stomach. She'd taken the day off. In fact she'd taken two. Unheard of. Now she was lazing around in bed past noon. What was with her?

Jeremy. His kiss. His hands on her body. His mouth on her skin. He was sexy, funny and...

And young.

She'd ask herself what did she think she was doing, but the tenderness of her breasts and the achiness between her thighs was a pretty good reminder.

She'd never been with anyone younger than her. Not even by a month. She didn't need to consult Dr. Freud to know it stemmed from watching her father date women who were less than his age. First five years. Then seven. Finally fifteen.

Damn, was she using Jeremy? Using him to make her feel good about getting older? About gravity? About a lot of things? Was she that far off from her father?

Jeremy rolled over, reaching for her in the dark. Grasping her breast. He smiled in his sleep as her nipple hardened against his palm. That wasn't the only thing hardening.

Even half-awake, he'd explored the terrain of her body with ease. His mouth had sought the sweet spot below her ear where she loved to have him kiss. Lick.

The way he made love to her was beautiful. The way he made her feel, amazing. She didn't want anything ugly between them. Anything that remotely resembled the kind of relationships her father had had with his younger women.

"Jeremy?" she whispered. If he didn't wake up, she could postpone this little conversation until morning.

He lifted his head. He smiled at her sleepily. "Is something wrong?" he asked, automatically reaching to comfort her.

She scooted away from him, as if she didn't quite

trust herself to get through this without dropping the whole subject so she could make love with him instead.

Okay, here it goes. "What do you see happening here?"

Jeremy nodded, as if he'd suspected this would occur. The mattress squeaked as he sat up and rubbed his eyes.

"A guy driving halfway across the country doesn't exactly speak one-night stand," she said quickly.

"The way you hightailed it out of my hotel room back home tells me you aren't looking for anything long-term." His tone had changed. Slightly negative.

Why should she be surprised? They'd shared a week-end of no-strings sex. Weren't twentysomething men supposed to be into that? And bonus, she'd left him before there could be any weird, awkward parting moments. There'd been no faux "Let's keep in touch" or uncomfortable hug. Leaving that way had done them both a favor. Right?

"It was best that way," she said quietly, dropping his gaze.

"For you?" But he wouldn't let her block him out. He reached for her hands, his body on edge. "Miriam, I was worried sick. I didn't even know if you'd made it home safely."

Something warm and gooey formed around her heart at his words. Yuck. She was a grown woman. Ran a business. She could take care of herself.

And yet, that yucky gooey feeling wasn't all that bad. It was kind of nice to think someone cared whether or not she was stranded by the side of the road. She couldn't help it. She smiled.

"I never thought you'd worry about me."

Some of the tension he'd carried in his shoulders relaxed. His lips turned up in a smile. "Well, I did." His gaze captured hers for a moment, and he swallowed.

"I haven't been able to stop thinking about you. Wondering what you were doing. When I forgot about the blind date my sister had set up, I knew I had to figure out what was going on between us. I'd never stand up another person. I felt terrible."

Miriam didn't. The idea of him being with another woman made her stomach clench, and she'd never been the jealous type. Not once. She'd read enough articles in her magazine to know jealousy was not a productive emotion. But then she'd never been so attuned to a man's every movement as she had been that weekend. And still was, based on their latest performance between the sheets.

"So, this trip is to get me out of your system?"

"The timing was right to see what we have. I'm between jobs right now."

Yes, of course he was. Dad's women never seemed to keep a job for long.

His hand settled on her thigh, sending shivers along her skin, and the fact that he didn't have a job wasn't such an issue at the moment.

"But given the last two days, it might take a long, long time before I get you out of my system." His hands cupped her hips and he lifted her to straddle him. He was already hard and ready for her, and her nipples tightened in anticipation of his touch. Jeremy was a breast man.

His fingers slid into her hair, and he gently drew her head toward him. "This can be whatever we want it to be," he whispered against her mouth.

TONIGHT IAN WAS TAKING her on a date. With him and nineteen other men. They were going on something called a speed date. Once again she had researched what she should wear, but the predominant answer was "business casual," and that was even more difficult to fathom than going out to a nightclub.

Finally she opted for a black calf-length skirt with a bit of a kick pleat at the bottom. Her top was a salmon-colored scoop-neck blouse with a business jacket in case she got cold.

She did a quick turn for Ian when she met him outside the Bricktown restaurant where the event would be held. "How do I look?"

"My sister would approve."

She lifted an eyebrow. "But you don't."

"Maybe I prefer paint."

Her skin flushed as she remembered the way she'd first presented herself to Ian. He'd liked what he'd seen and she reveled in it now. Suddenly she didn't want to "date" anyone. Even if it were for seven minutes at a time.

Right now she just wanted to get to know Ian better. Away from her book. Away from customs. Just the way normal North American men and women met one another.

Unfortunately, speed dating seemed to be the way they did it. What a strange social rite. "How did this whole system develop?" she asked as he opened the door for her.

"Look at us. We spent a lot of our time in school, then out in the field with our careers. A person wakes up one day and realizes they forgot to date. So here's the most efficient way to meet people who might be about your same age, experience and education, who have the same problem."

Ian led her into a banquet room with a large sign proclaiming Speed Daters Welcome.

"Men on the left, women on the right," came the loud voice of a woman standing on a chair and calling to them from the other side of a bullhorn.

"Have fun," Ian said as he made his way to the left, and she joined a group of women dressed similarly to her. Whew, she hadn't blown that.

"We'll take a few moments to get everyone checked in with their name tags in place. There's wine at the front of the room, may I suggest you partake of it?" said the woman with the bullhorn.

Several of the people laughed and made their way toward the wine table. Five minutes later, she was in her seat, sporting her name tag, as well as the number eighteen, just in case the man couldn't remember her name. She had a score sheet and a pen, and was armed with strict instructions not to write anything down until after she'd been on all the dates.

"When I blow my whistle, the men move to the left. Please do this quickly as we only have the room until nine. Let's begin."

A nice-looking man of about thirty or so sat across from her first. He had a sweet, friendly smile. "Hi, I'm Zach. So, do you want to have children in the future?"

Ava found herself longing for the whistle.

Luckily Ian was her fifth "date." "How is it going?" he asked.

"This feels more like a job interview than dating. I've been asked about my religion, my sexual health and my politics."

"Well, you're interviewing each other for the job of significant other."

"Sounds inspiring."

"Do I detect a note of disdain? From the woman who has no problem with a bunch of men wearing penis carvings around their necks, this, *this* is what you find unusual?"

"It's so clinical."

"Remember what you said about how most problems between a man and a woman could be solved with just a simple conversation? Think about how easy it would be if you had all potential dating landmines already out in the open?"

She hated to admit it, but he did have a point. And using her own words against her. How irritating.

The whistle sounded and Ian stood. He was successful. He was smart and funny, and in his chinos and long-sleeved polo shirt he was amazingly handsome. The epitome of what a twenty-first-century woman should want.

And although she sometimes dabbled in ancient

cultures, she was all twenty-first-century woman to-night. She'd much rather spend the next seven minutes and the seven minutes after that talking with Ian. Laughing with Ian. That initial physical attraction she'd felt for him was beginning to deepen. She was beginning to want more.

She suffered through the next few men, all decent guys, but biology did strange things to a person. Not one of them seemed as interesting as Ian. Her body had found her bedmate for the time being. It just took her mind a bit to catch up.

Finally the last whistle sounded and they were free to fill out their cards. She only marked Ian's name and number. They were free to mingle for a few minutes longer while the organizers compared cards and readied contact information. She opted for another glass of wine.

One of the organizers came by and handed them each an envelope. "How'd you do?" he asked.

Her sheet was blank. "Not one request. I must have been putting out the wrong vibes."

He flashed her an incredulous look.

"I didn't even score your number."

"You already have my number."

"How'd you do?"

Ian folded the piece of paper and tucked it into his back pocket. "Doesn't matter."

"Ian."

"Fifteen."

"Fifteen?" she asked loudly, her voice drawing the attention of several of the other daters.

Ian laughed. "Come on, I'll walk you back to your apartment."

"Wait a minute, these were only mutual requests. You would have had to list them as wanting their contact information, as well."

"All in the interest of research. I'm sure you can appreciate that."

"Sounds like a male ego needing a few strokes to me," she grumbled.

"Hey, a man's got to take them when he can. The last woman I kissed blew me off for the sake of a book," he said good-naturedly.

She laughed, and they walked along the canal together, the lights reflecting in the water. This being a weeknight, there wasn't much foot traffic, and the boats that floated along the canal were docked for the night.

"Ian, after this book is over, what do you plan to do?" she asked.

He ran a hand through his hair, and looked away as if he hadn't thought much past the book and it shocked him. "Guess I'll head for whichever hot spot is calling and my sister wants covered."

They walked in silence for a moment, the breeze turning cooler.

"What about you?" he asked and for the first time she heard hesitancy in his voice.

"Maybe start working on some ideas for a new book. Send out my résumé to a few colleges. But I'd really like to take a few weeks off. Take a vacation and just look around at all of what I've missed."

They rounded the corner to her apartment building. She stood on the first step and turned, staring at him eye to eye.

"Been a while since I took a vacation myself," he said.

Ava's heart quickened its pace. She couldn't prevent the huge smile on her face. He reached up and cupped her cheek, his thumb stroking her bottom lip.

This was the playacting he'd been talking about earlier. The kind he said he was used to. She should look at him and say, "Ian, after this book is over, I'd like to spend more time with you." But for some reason that scared the crap out of her. It was way scarier than telling a man you wanted him sexually.

Her eyes closed and she leaned into him. Ian met her halfway. His lips were now familiar to her. Wanted. His kiss was quick, firm and filled with promise. Then, with a final caress to her cheek, he took a step away.

"Good night, Ava."

He stayed on her stoop until he saw her key into her apartment building. After making sure the door behind her had closed fully, Ava made her way up the stairs to the top floor slowly. She was really rethinking her decision from earlier not to self-pleasure. Her nipples tightened just from her slipping the jacket she'd worn to the restaurant off her shoulders.

In her bedroom, she let her thumbs stroke down the swell of her breasts, circling around the tips. She sucked in a breath, imagining Ian's hands removing her bra. Ian's fingers teasing her nipples.

But no, she'd made a decision to keep the sexual tension high, and an orgasm now would surely lessen the heat between them.

Instead she tried to focus on all things cold. Feeling a little less heated, she kicked off her shoes, slid out of her skirt and blouse and zipped up one of the ceremonial robes she'd picked up from a Polynesian island late last year.

How long she paced in front of her floor-to-ceiling bookcase in agitation she didn't know. Her shoulders were tense, her brow was furrowed, her stomach was tight…and not in a good way. She should burn some incense. Some nice aromatherapy should really make her relax. But after a quick look through her scents, she realized every one of them was geared toward awakening sexual sensations, not relaxing.

They'd be working on the food section next. Maybe she could start preparing some of the more exotic fare.

With a smile, Ava stopped her pacing. She didn't need to concentrate on not thinking about sex, but instead work on filling her thoughts with something completely different. She ran her fingers along some of her books, but not even those dear friends could take her mind off the heat in her blood. That man was a dangerous kisser.

At least she'd given as good as she'd got. She'd spotted the regretful ardor in his brown eyes before she walked away. She'd felt the hard ridge of his penis against her belly. If they could transfer all that sexual tension and passion onto the pages of her book, it would ignite. It might even make her a bestseller.

Her phone rang, and she jumped. Fewer than five people had her number, and—she glanced at the ornamental clock her brother had given her—and it was almost two in the morning.

"Hello," she said, a little hesitantly.

"I was lying here on my bed in the dark, thinking how stupid I was leaving you after that kiss."

Ava smiled into the phone.

"You there?" Ian asked.

"Well, I'm not going to argue with you."

Ian laughed. "I was thinking that instead of kissing you goodbye, you would have asked me upstairs. Maybe offered me coffee."

"Would I really make it?" she asked.

"No. That was just an excuse to get me to come up to your apartment so we could be together."

"Do we need an *excuse?*"

"Ahh, good question. No, but twenty-first-century couples don't just come out and say, 'Why don't you come upstairs with me so we can neck?' We have to be way more restrained than that. Part of the pretending stuff I was telling you about."

"But why? We're living in one of the most liberated times and places of the ages."

"It's the power thing we talked about. The battle lines. You don't tell a woman you're falling for her. Women play hard to get. Men wait two days before calling a woman once he's got her number."

She swallowed. Was Ian falling for her? Or was he just talking in the abstract? Of course it was in the abstract.

"So where does the coffee thing come in?" she asked.

"Sometimes you want to break the rules."

"So new rules were invented. Another dance, but each knows what the step really means." Now this was making more sense to her.

"Exactly. You pretend you're really going to make us something to drink. I pretend I'm interested in drinking it. Instead you're in my arms."

Ava closed her eyes at the idea of being in Ian's arms again. Of kiss— Of necking with Ian on her couch.

"So we missed that opportunity."

"Maybe that particular opportunity, but there is something else we can do. Tell me what you're wearing."

"What?" That was the last thing she'd expected him to say.

"You tell me what you're wearing. Your voice turns all soft and low, like you're half a second away from moaning. You tell me what you like. Where you want me to touch you. I respond by telling you what I'm doing to your body. This is what we call phone sex."

"You're kidding, right?" She'd studied some unusual ways to avoid approaching a potential suitor from her days as an intern on assignment. Anything from having a brother or uncle ask the groom's intended bride for her hand in marriage on his behalf, or the ghost marriage, where the wedded couple never even met until after some type of sign from long-dead relatives that the union was sound. But sex was always done together and in the actual physical presence and with the other person.

"No, I'm serious. And if you study closely, I'm going to rock your world."

She laughed because this guy knew a word like *study* would really attract her attention. "You just had to put it like that."

"I know your inquisitive mind couldn't stand *not* knowing something that has to do with sexual customs."

Her heartbeat quickened. For the first time she was with a man who truly understood what made her excited and grabbed her attention. "Well, bring it on," she invited.

"Tell me what you're wearing."

13

THIS WAS SUPPOSED to rock her world? Although she doubted anything would come from it, she said, "I went upstairs, and changed into something that originates from Hawaii."

She heard him swallow. "Describe it."

Ava glanced down, a little confused. Ian seemed a little more interested in female clothing than most of her male acquaintances. "Bright pink and white flowers. They're very large, but you can still see the canary color of the background material. The costume hangs straight from my shoulders."

"What the—? Are you telling me you're wearing a mu—"

"A muumuu. It's a traditional gown, which is quite comfortable."

"I know what a muumuu is." Ian cleared his throat. "It's very eye-catching."

"I can imagine that it is," he said drily. "When you mentioned Hawaii, I was imagining a grass skirt and a coconut shell top."

She laughed. "You imagine like a tourist. And

although Hawaiian residents prefer more muted colors than what I'm wearing, this is pretty standard. I love the puffy sleeves."

"Keep talking about it. It's turning me the hell on."

"Turning you on?" Was *that* what she was supposed to be doing here when describing her clothes? Her breath came out in a frustrated sigh. She'd totally missed that. And she didn't usually miss that stuff. "Ah. Let me try this again."

Ava grabbed the zipper on her muumuu and tugged, lowering the phone downward as she progressed. "Did you hear that?"

There was another long pause.

"Ian?"

"Yes." His voice sounded like pure agonized strain.

Ava grinned. "Thought I'd lost you there."

"You almost did."

Her smile turned contemplative. She loved his honesty. "From the sound of things a moment ago, you didn't think my dress was all that sexy," Ava said, the teasing tone now gone.

"Since I met this seductive researcher, a lot of things I didn't realize were sexy are pretty damn incredible."

Her heart almost slammed into her ribs. All night they'd been playing games, flirting with each other. The dance, the back and forth of courtship. But now, in the early-morning hours they'd finally arrived at the real truth. He wanted her. She wanted him.

She couldn't explain why, but then she really had no urge to. Who a person desired, what made a woman crave a man's touch, what made a man hunger to wrap a specific woman in his arms rarely made sense on a logical level. She'd been studying it long enough to know that.

Ian made her burn. Made her nipples ache for his touch, her skin yearn for his caresses. And despite him leaving her on the stoop earlier this evening, Ian wanted her. The signs were all there. The way his pulse had beat at his temple. The way his brown eyes slightly dilated when he looked at her.

It didn't make sense to want this man. He wasn't an academic, didn't share her interests and looked at her work with a good dose of skepticism. But pheromones and biology said *take this man. Now.*

She didn't have an urge to make it logical.

Ava simply accepted it.

Now she'd embrace it.

The man had suggested that phone sex was twenty-first-century foreplay. She was a researcher…she should experience it. Okay, not right. She wouldn't use that as an excuse to take part. Justification was a strange thing. Sprang up of its own free will. Ava wouldn't rationalize wanting Ian. She'd just go with it.

"Tell me how we get started," she told him. Her voice husky and filled with invitation.

"Tell me where you are."

"I'm in my living room, looking out the window."

"Are you looking toward my hotel? Were you thinking of me before I called?"

"Well, I was thinking of you, but I had no idea where your hotel is."

"It's west of you."

Ava shook her head as she looked out into the night, not even bothering to guess which way was west. "Still not helping."

"North, south, east, west—all simple concepts. Why is it that women can never seem to 'get' directions?"

"Because we didn't need to. Men have to know stuff like herds move north in the fall. As a woman, I just needed to remember that the edible roots usually grow right next to the bush with the pretty blue flowers. Don't worry, you tell me what your hotel is next to, I'll find you."

"Seems like an imprecise way of traveling around. Although I like the sound of you finding me."

"Don't knock it. Sometimes my roots and nuts will save your meat-hunting backside. Survival is a team effort."

"Ready to win one for the team now?"

Her brows knitted in confusion. "Uh…sure?"

"That's an expression, Ava. Sometimes I forget you weren't raised here."

"So winning one for the team means something like giving us both pleasure?"

"Something like that," he said, his voice turning gruff. "Forget the window stuff, just go to your bedroom."

Ava took the few steps down the hallway and into her bedroom. "I'm here."

"Set the scene. Describe it to me."

She glanced around the room, trying to see it through his eyes. "I've painted it a rich, dark green. It reminds me of some of my favorite places I've studied. I have plants all around, small palms and orchids. Waking up to the sweet smell of flowers is one of life's pleasures, don't you think?"

"One of them," he answered.

"I have a sweep of tulle making a canopy. It just didn't feel right sleeping without netting."

"Your bed, Ava. Tell me about your bed," he said, his voice raspy.

She shivered, anticipating how she'd describe it to him. "It's pure indulgence. After sleeping in sleeping bags and cots, I opted to pamper myself. I splurged on one of those pillowtop mattresses. When I lie down on it, I feel like I'm lying on a soft cloud."

"Lie on it now." His voice was a rough command.

Her footfalls were almost silent as she stepped across the hardwood floor. She stretched out against the silken khaki fabric. The material was cool, but her blood ran hot.

"How does it feel against your skin?" Ian asked.

"Cool and smooth. My comforter is silk, another indulgence, but I couldn't resist."

He chuckled. A sensual sound that seemed to come from deep inside his body. She responded to the earthiness of it, her skin growing flushed.

"I like that about you," he said. "I don't want you to resist a thing. Rub the material against your skin."

Ava lifted a corner of her comforter and ran the silky material along the curve of her neck, and moaned into the phone.

She may have heard him groan. "That's it, Ava. Tell me how it feels as you're doing it. Touch your breasts."

She heard the ache in his voice. The need. Her nipples tightened, and she grew wet.

"The fabric was cool at first as I touched my skin, but my body heat has made it warmer. I'm tracing the outline of my nipple. I'm watching it get hard."

"You don't turn off the lights?" he asked.

"Why would I?"

He chuckled again, but it sounded more like an agonized groan. "Not a reason I can think of. Touch yourself with your hands."

"Where?" she asked, not able to resist a small tease.

"Between your legs, but get there slowly."

Dropping the comforter, Ava cupped her breasts. Tweaked her nipples with her thumbs. "My breasts feel heavier. Warmer. They ache to be caressed. Kissed." *By him.*

This time Ian did groan. "Go lower."

Ava wound a wavy path down her rib cage. Her stomach muscles quivered under her fingertips. She'd gone down this path on her body before. Many times. But the sensations were more taut this time. That much more sweet.

"I've come to my panties." Her fingers were toying with the elastic at her hips.

"What color are they?"

"Red."

"My new favorite color. Touch yourself through them."

"Through them?" Surely he meant *under* them. The

rushing of her blood in her ears must be making him hard to hear.

"Yes, through them. That's how I'd start. I'd stroke you over those sexy red panties of yours until…"

Her toes curled into the mattress at his words. She slipped her hand down over her body, down past the elastic of her waistband. Ava's hand went lower until her fingertips rested between her legs.

"I'm there," she said, breathless. Wanting so much more. Waiting for what he'd say next. Wondering what he'd have her do next.

"Run your finger along yourself. Along the folds of your skin. Gently. Get yourself used to my touch."

Ava's eyes squeezed tight. Ian had just made it personal, told her how he'd like to touch her. Her legs began to quiver.

She followed his instruction, skimming her flesh. With a tiny gasp, she arched into her hand.

"How does that feel?" he asked.

"Good. So good." Her breath coming out in little pants.

"I think you can do better than that," he said. "You get to feel. I want to hear."

"It feels amazing, but I want more. I need more."

"That's good." The utter satisfaction she heard in his voice made her smile, despite her blood feeling on fire. "Circle around your clit. Don't touch, just circle."

Ava traced around the small area, her body growing tighter in anticipation. "Is this the way you'd touch me?" It was hard to get the words out, she was so lost in the pleasure.

"Yes," he said, his voice clipped and filled with hunger. "When I know you're ready for more, that's when I slide my hand down inside your panties."

"Do you like that?"

"Nothing compares to following that path down your body. Feeling the heat of you against my hand. The wetness that tells me how much you want me. Slip a finger inside, Ava."

She felt the warmth, the wetness. Her hips rose to meet her finger.

"Are you imagining it's me?" he asked.

"Yes," she hissed. The word long and drawn out. She was close, so close to coming.

"Imagine me taking off your panties."

"How?" she asked. But whatever way it was, she only knew she'd want it to be fast.

"Maybe with my hands. Maybe with my teeth."

She sucked in a breath, the image of his dark head down between her legs drawing her closer and closer to orgasm.

If Ian had simply told her what phone sex was in a casual conversation, she would never have guessed a man and a woman could get such pleasure out of the act. There seemed to be a lack of connection and visual stimulation.

But experiencing it was something completely different. Hearing Ian's voice across the line, hearing how her words and actions affected him, it was very, very sexy.

Ava pulled her hands from her body and wiggled out of her panties. She tossed them to the side and snuggled under the comforter.

"Are your panties off?" he asked, his voice desperate, as though he needed to know. Had to know.

"Yes."

"Now I touch your clit. How would you want it, Ava? With my finger or with my tongue?"

"Both," she said. Her voice nothing but a moan.

"Greedy." He gave her that sexy chuckle. "I'll remember that. I appreciate a woman who enjoys oral, who's not afraid to talk about it."

He'd found the right woman.

"Touch your clit."

Ava circled around it for a moment, then found the exact right spot. She gasped.

"It feels good, doesn't it Ava?"

She nodded, so close. So very close to exploding right there with just his rich, sexy voice to urge her on.

"Imagine me touching you. Gripping you by the hips and sliding inside you."

"Oh, yes." Her muscles flexed. Her body strained.

"In and out I'd stroke. I'm caressing your breasts, licking the side of your neck."

Her motions on her body became quicker, her fingers more urgent.

"And right when you're about to come, I'd kiss you. I want to feel your gasp of pleasure with my lips. Come for me now, Ava. Come now."

She gave into his words. Her senses exploded. Her pleasure arriving in wave after wave of tingles, shivers and tremors. "Ian," she moaned.

"That's it, Ava. I love hearing you say my name like

that as you hit. Don't hold back. I want to hear every sound you make."

The intensity of her orgasm and his words were overwhelming. Her voice loud. Her body tense and tight. Finally, finally the sensations ebbed. Her hair clung to her face, the sheets tangled about her feet as she'd thrashed on the bed.

"Did you enjoy that, Ava?"

"Yes," she told him, her voice still weak.

"I'll see you in the morning. Good night," he said softly. His voice was like another caress against her overheated and sensitive skin.

"But you didn't get—" But the hum of the dial tone told her he'd already hung up.

Confusion assailed her. Reaching below her feet, Ava tugged the sheets around her body. Her skin still so sensitive to the touch.

She curled into a tight ball.

In protection?

She wouldn't doubt it. She needed something like that right now. Because there was something else biology gave a woman. The knowledge of when to guard herself from certain heartbreak.

And in spite of the pleasure Ian's sexy voice promised, the heartbreak was there, as well.

14

Ava PREPARED the scene carefully. Today was the first ritual she'd be working on with Ian on a one-on-one basis. She hadn't expected to use this one today, but after the night she'd spent with Ian, the unselfish pleasure he'd given her last night, this ceremony seemed perfect.

Although she'd still take heed of the warning signals her body had sent off last night.

The oils and foods had been easy enough. The fresh flowers had been a bit hard to secure on such short notice in the wintertime, but she liked the effect of the deep purple carnations. With the help of a ladder, she'd managed to drape fabric over the windows and across the ceiling, using the ductwork.

Her front room had the very secluded, enclosed intimacy of a hut.

She'd forgone the fire for obvious reasons, but the couples using her book could easily recreate the Dravonian Sending-Off Ceremony environment with various candles, the way she'd done.

After she sliced open several black trash bags, her setting was complete.

"What's with all the plastic on the floor?" Ian asked as he finished setting up his camera.

The man had been all business since arriving at her apartment this morning. Not a word about what had happened late last night. His attitude put her mind at ease that they could remain professional and still be sensual together.

"Oh, it's to protect the hardwood from all the oil."

His hand slipped on the tripod. "Oil?" he asked.

She touched the bag with her bare, red-tipped toe, and eyed him seductively. "A trash bag isn't the most sensual or arousing prop I could have used, but it's easily accessible for most women."

"Did you say oil?"

Ava nodded. "Yes, for the massage. This is the Hero Send-Off. You may remember from my first draft that all the ceremonies in the book are for couples, so they can achieve the ultimate pleasure for both parties."

She made a show of fluffing up the flowers, trying to hide her attempt at gauging Ian's reaction. Although she'd appreciated his professional behavior, it kind of irked her on some level. "You remember, pleasure for both, right?" Her voice lower now.

Ian nodded, then returned his attention to his light gauge or whatever he was fiddling with. His movements were choppy, his motions clipped.

That was more like it.

"But this is the Hero Send-Off. The Dravonian culture has died off now, but we know a lot of their traditions by their extensive cave drawings discovered in eastern Europe." She found herself fingering the props as she watched him finish with his equipment.

"We suspect that the Send-Off developed during times of war, when clashing tribes fought over territory. But with the domestication of some plants, the tribes began to merge, and the women's traditions for sending off their men moved to right before the last prewinter hunt." Ian completed his tasks, and walked toward her. Reluctantly, almost as if he didn't want to get near her.

She'd take that as a good sign. "Of course the hunt was not as dangerous as going off to fight, but who could blame the men for not wanting to lose out on that particular practice?"

Ian shook his head, his brown eyes scanning the scene she'd set. "No, I can't see any man wanting to give all this up." Then his gaze returned to hers. Heated and curious—her favorite combination.

She had his attention now. Ian was clearly intrigued about what kind of send-off the women would give their men. "Can you take pictures in the hut I made? I think any shots in there would be more effective in explaining the atmosphere to readers."

"Shouldn't be a problem."

"Good. Though I don't want it to seem like I'm discounting the dangers of the last hunt. It was far more dangerous than others. The men would be competing for game with other predators, and the meat would be so important to sustain the tribe through the winter."

A smile tugged at Ian's lips and her heart did a tiny

flip-flop. "Told you something more was needed than just fruits and nuts," he teased.

"Yes, the men's contribution was very important. Step inside the hut, and I'll show you how the women prepared their men."

The laughter left Ian's eyes. *Yeah, that will show you to try and tease me.*

With a shrug, the robe Ava had been wearing slipped off her shoulders. The air was cool against her nearly naked skin. "The idea was to surround the man with his favorites. His woman would greet him in what she knew he liked to see her in. I didn't know for sure what you preferred, but you seemed to enjoy my loincloth."

Ian's breath came out in a hiss as the robe fell to the floor. She adjusted the straps at her hips. She'd paired it with a matching beaded top, replacing the paint from a week ago. "If you were facing danger tomorrow, maybe even death, is this what you'd like to see me in the night before?"

Ian nodded, not able to take his eyes off her body.

Satisfied with his reaction, Ava sank to her knees and crawled into the hut she'd made. Ian followed, keeping his distance. A pretty impressive move when her make-shift hut was less than four feet wide.

Her voice dipped low. "The whole point was to make him feel important. Loved and yet invincible. As if he could face and conquer anything come the next sunrise. The woman would take away all his worry, to give him the opportunity to relax, not to think. Whatever her man most desires before he heads off to the hunt."

"You know, if you want, I could go get us some steaks."

Ava laughed low in her throat. She saw the naked desire on Ian's face now. She met his eyes. "Although it seems only beneficial to the man, the woman enjoys it, too. This might be her last night with the one she loves. How better than to spend it in only…pleasure?"

"None better."

"Let's start with the oil." She uncapped the bottle, and poured a generous amount in her hand, warming it between her fingers.

Ian's eyes followed her every movement, and he licked his lips.

"Aren't you going to join me?"

His gaze met hers. "What?"

"I think these pictures would be more effective if they show me demonstrating on a man's body."

"I have to take the pictures."

"Isn't there some sort of autosnap? Come here. How are you supposed to write it without experiencing it yourself? When you think you have a good shot, set it up, then come back."

He paused for a moment, then he nodded. "That might work." He turned his gaze to hers, and she almost gasped at the look of anguished desire displayed in those brown depths.

Ian had the distinct look of a man who didn't want her to touch him. She could only guess he was a man used to being in charge. Too bad. Last night he'd driven her to distraction. That's what she wanted to give him this morning.

His arms slumped to his sides and he crawled toward her.

"You'll need to take off your shirt."

"Why?"

Yeah, that was her question. Why all the reluctance? "Is there a way I could give you a massage with your shirt on?"

With a shrug, Ian lifted his shirt over his head, and tossed it out the opening of her tent.

It was her turn to be reluctant. Ian had the kind of body that drove women to create ceremonies like the Send-Off. He was a man who lived in the field, worked hard with his body, and it showed. He didn't have the bulk of someone who worked for those muscles in a gym. No, his body was lean strength, tight stomach and hardened pecs. A light smattering of hair led temptingly lower.

Her fingers itched to touch his skin. Caress his muscles. She swallowed over the hard lump in her throat. She knew her body must be flashing all the signals of an aroused woman. She felt the blush above her breasts. Knew her nipples were poking at the material of her top.

His gaze turned heated, and she saw his hands fist and flex at his side.

"It's okay, Ian. I'll make sure you enjoy this."

"That's what I'm afraid of," he stated. This was no soft utterance or muttering under his breath. It was that amazing honesty from yesterday. His words made her burn.

Ian was done hiding his desire and also obviously through with masking his reluctance, too. Could his

hesitation be rooted in the same reasons as her own pro-
active gestures of last night?

They wanted each other, but were both clearly cautious.
She'd never shied away from anything, and she doubted
the alpha loner in front of her had, either. Why now?

As a researcher, she'd love to ponder and contemplate
the reasons until she came up with a reasonable answer.
As a woman, she just wanted her hands on his body.

"Your pants, too."

He raised an eyebrow.

"It's going to get really oily in here, do you want that
on your khakis?"

Ian's fingers moved to the button, and unhooked it.
Then he found the zipper, his eyes never leaving her
face. But she was too curious, so her gaze slid downward. She sucked in a breath as she realized something
about Ian. He didn't like to wear underwear.

The pants slid down his legs, revealing a deep tan
with none of the telltale marks of a man who wore
trunks when he swam. Already semierect, he was impressive to behold.

She recognized her age-old womanly response. Her
lips parted. Her breasts felt heavy.

His pants soon joined his shirt outside the material
walls. Ian turned, presenting her his back. Smooth and
tanned and muscled, it matched the rest of his body.

The skin of his shoulders quivered as she placed her
oil-ready hands on him. His hot flesh felt right beneath
her fingertips. "You seem tense," she said.

"Getting tenser by the moment."

She smiled, her skin becoming more sensitive as she grew aroused. Ava began to rub and knead his flesh. "There's no record that the Dravonian women had any special techniques. I think they just did whatever made the man feel good. Does this make you feel good, Ian?"

"Yes." His voice was low and huskier than before.

Done with his shoulders, she poured more oil into her hand. She slid her hands down his spine, watching him flex and move under her ministrations.

She cupped the firmness of his backside. He had the perfect butt, and his muscles grew more taut as she worked him.

"This doesn't seem to be doing the trick of relaxing you. Maybe this will help."

Ava reached behind her and tugged the bow at her neck holding the halter top in place. The bow between her shoulder blades was more tricky with her fingers so slippery, but she managed to get it undone, too.

Her top fell to the protected floor with a whoosh. Ian shifted around to see what had fallen. His eyes widened at the sight of her nearly naked body.

Ava's nipples hardened further under his gaze. She poured more oil into her hands and rubbed it all over her breasts, loving the slick feeling against her sensitive flesh.

"I suspect that after a while the woman did something like this." Ava cupped her body to Ian's back, rubbing her oil-glazed body against his skin. The sensation was amazing. Unlike any she'd felt before.

She began to run her fingers up and down the sides of his body. His thighs. His ribs. With each stroke downward, his frame jerked as she found her fingers closer and closer to his penis.

She would have loved to have done this last night. Touched him for real, instead of in her imagination.

The oil was working its magic. His skin glistened in the candlelight. Finally the slickness became too much and he fell, his arms barely bracing both of them.

"Roll onto your back. I think it's time to massage your front," she urged.

Ian circled to his back, bringing her along with him. "Never understood the appeal of oil-wrestling until now," he said.

"What?"

Ian shook his head. "I'll explain it later. I like what you're doing now."

She smiled, and poured more oil into her hands, rubbing to heat up the liquid. Then she smoothed it onto his chest, running her fingers along his collarbone, his nipples and the muscled lines of his stomach.

When she settled on his hips, his cock jutted forward. Her gaze lowered. His hard length was ready for anything she wanted to give him.

Ava suddenly held a new appreciation for the control Dravonian women must have had. Her skin screamed for his touch. His caresses. His mouth on her body.

She could only imagine how intense the experience would be for a woman who was loved by the man beside her, and her fearing for his safety. Everything, every touch, every taste, every sense would be heightened.

She needed to take a breather, to get her riotous body

more in check. "I have some sliced meats and some tra-ditional bite-sized boiled potatoes. Usually the woman feeds her man."

"Nice to know meat-and-potato men always existed."

"What?"

Ian groaned deep in his throat. "No, ignore me. I don't want you to feed me. In fact, I don't want you to stop what you're doing at all. And in case that's not clear enough, I want your sexy little hands back on my body. Touching me. Stroking me."

Her hand reached for the base of his cock. "Like this?" she asked.

He shivered below her, his face a beautiful picture of male concentration.

"Yes," he answered, his voice barely above a whisper.

Ava wrapped her fingers around his shaft, then slow-ly raised her hand to the tip, the oil making the move-ment easy and smooth.

His hips lifted, and she caressed the tip of him with her thumb. Then she lowered her hand down his shaft.

His eyes flew open. "Ava, that feels so good."

She lowered her lips to give him a quick kiss. "Enjoy it," she said against his mouth. "I am."

Ava began to move up and down his cock, gradually increasing her speed. The muscles of his stomach flexed and his thighs shook. His hands came up to grip her. To stop her. "Ava."

She shook her head. "No, let me do this. You gave to me last night. Let me give to you now."

The hands that had come up to stop her movements,

embraced her. Helped her find the rhythm he liked best. She watched his face, fascinated by the tightness of his jaw. The candlelight exposing the strength of his re-action to her touch.

He grew harder in her hand.

Her heart beat faster in eagerness. She knew his orgasm was near, and she couldn't wait to watch him. The core of her ached to have him feel her, but she resisted the urge to rub her clit against his hair-roughened but oil-slick thigh. That would be strictly against the rules of the ceremony.

Instead, she put even more effort into her ministra-tions to Ian's body. She rode her hand up and down his shaft, using her thumb to tease the head of him.

With a groan that tore from somewhere deep inside him, Ian came.

She couldn't wait to make him do it again.

15

THE LIGHT ABOVE the breakfast bar in Miriam's apartment flashed off and on. "Oh, I can't believe it. I've called that in. The super told me he'd fixed it."

Jeremy looked above his head. "It's probably just a loose connection. I'll take a look at it after breakfast."

She flashed him a skeptical look. "Don't worry about it. I hire someone to take care of things like that."

He glanced upwards again. "Really, I could check that in a minute."

"There you go again, trying to save me. Honestly, the last thing I want you doing is wasting your time here with me fixing stuff."

His neck reddened. How she loved that about him. It was as if he was slightly embarrassed by their reaction to one another.

"When you put it like that…" Jeremy finished off the omelet Miriam had made him, and set the plate aside. "This was great. Thanks."

Miriam smiled, pleased she'd satisfied one of his hungers. "Glad you enjoyed them. Scrambling eggs is about the only domestic thing I do."

He stood, lifting his plate off the counter. "In that case, I wash and dry. You can sit down."

Wash and dry? By hand? What kind of person did he think she was? Miriam waved his comment away. "Just stack it in the sink. I have someone that comes in every morning to tidy up and prepare a meal for dinner. Takeout gets old."

"You're missing out on one of life's greatest times between two people." His blue eyes grew darker. "Outside of bed."

"Takeout?"

Jeremy shook his head. "Dishwashing. My dad insists it's the key to a happy marriage."

Another knock against the institution. Besides, Miriam couldn't fathom for a moment how dishwashing could be in any way joyful. Housework equaled drudgery in her mind.

"I can see from your face you're skeptical. Every night after dinner, my dad would wash and my mom would dry. They'd talk about their day, the meal, whatever. I could usually hear laughter coming from the kitchen."

Miriam squirmed in her chair, uncomfortable with where this conversation was leading. The illusion of martial bliss. "Couldn't they do other things together?"

"I don't think it's the same. Last year, I bought them a dishwasher for their anniversary. I think mom uses it during the day or on holidays, but for the most part, it's them together at night."

Her eyes widened. What was wrong with these people? "I still don't get it."

"I didn't, either. My father told me it's one of those tasks that your body can do on autopilot. So you talk. You're close, and you stand side by side. The way a relationship should be."

This kind of reminded her of the doc's writing that Ian had been sending to her via e-mail. About how generations of men and women spent time together quietly, doing little more than just being together. How going through life's journey seemed somehow easier when completed with someone you love.

Miriam smiled at him, but for some reason felt melancholy. Wow, happy parents in a happy marriage. Who knew they still existed? Certainly none of her friends came from any intact home life.

She was struck, and not for the first time, by how different she and Jeremy really were from each other. Oh, they connected in bed on a level that was beyond believing, but out of bed?

They were so very different, and not only the age thing. She'd graduated from Wharton, ran a company. Jeremy didn't even have a job, and didn't show much of an inclination to search for one, either.

He believed in domestic bliss.

Her business published articles on flings and long-distance relationships.

He—

The telephone interrupted her thoughts. Jeremy handed her the portable phone, his fingers caressing her hand. She decided right there and then she'd get rid of whoever was on the other end of the line. Fast. "Hello."

"So, tell me immediately why you are still not at work." It was Jenna, Miriam's best friend. Best friend and she still hadn't told her about Jeremy. Not about the weekend in Oklahoma, and not about now, either.

"I was due a break." And Jeremy was the long, tall vacation she'd needed. She watched him as he straightened up in the kitchen, running a damp paper towel over the counters she'd left covered in crumbs.

She could watch him unobserved. Jeremy looked fantastic this morning, shirtless and with his dark hair mussed. A flutter of desire began to unwind inside her. Not a bad way to start her morning.

"I'm coming over there."

Miriam whirled away from the sight of Jeremy in her kitchen, trying not to panic. "No, you can't. I mean—"

"Miriam Cole, what is going on over there? Are you sick? Running away from the law? Have a naked man tucked away folding your towels?"

Miriam gasped. Close. Almost naked and cleaning her kitchen.

"You naughty girl, you have someone there right now."

"No," she insisted. In full panic mode.

Jenna snorted. "Okay, however you want to play it. I expect all the juicy details later. Hey, bring him along tonight."

Oh, damn. This was the night of her monthly book club meeting. It was *Pride and Prejudice,* and at her suggestion. She could talk about that book for hours. And despite that it provided not one, but two romantic endings, sometimes she yearned for a time in her life when she believed in love.

Yes, she could talk about that book for hours, but she'd rather be with Jeremy. And it didn't matter what they were doing, in bed, out of bed, he beat out Jane Austen.

Her heart raced. She was getting in deeper than she'd thought. *Remember the article.* The odds of a long-distance relationship working weren't high. That's when she realized she'd secretly been hoping...what? That they could have something that lasted? The idea didn't make sense.

"I'm going to have to cancel out on you tonight," Miriam said slowly, not happy with the way her heart was turning against her logic.

Jenna made a sound. "I understand. Jane Austen not his scene? Bring him around later. I'm making fondue."

"I'll let you know."

"Wow. That means no, and that you're having great sex. Well, at least one of us is. Enjoy it, Mir."

Miriam replaced the receiver in the charger and took a deep breath. What was she doing? Why was she breaking long-standing commitments for a short-term love affair?

For just one second, she'd almost taken Jenna up on her offer to bring Jeremy over. And then it hit her...how could she take Jeremy? He had little enough in common with her, let alone her friends. He was more than fifteen years younger than any of them.

Which raised the question again, just what was she doing? They'd avoided any real discussion of where their relationship was going. Correction, she'd side-stepped Jeremy's every attempt to bring it up.

He'd said earlier he was game for wherever she saw it headed, and she was holding him to that. But the nagging fact remained, there was some real intimacy here between them, and she didn't want to examine their relationship too deeply.

She dropped her head into her palms.

Strong hands gently rested on her shoulders. "Everything okay?" Jeremy asked.

She nodded, not turning around. "Sure." *I'm just starting to act really irrationally around you. Because of you.*

He tenderly spun her to face him. "I couldn't help overhearing. You know, you don't have to change your routine just because I'm here. I know you have a life. I can head back to my hotel, and—"

Her lips stopped his words. It took him a moment to respond, her actions probably shocked him. Then he hauled her up tight against his chest and deepened the kiss with his tongue.

She pulled back to suck in a breath. "Make love to me, Jeremy."

IAN RINSED OFF ALL the oil from his body in Ava's shower. He'd invited her in, but she'd shaken her head and given him a wink. That wink told him all he needed to know. Later. They'd be together later. Why did she want to wait?

He knew it'd be sensational. And that loincloth

would play a large role in it. After last night's episode on the phone, he'd tried to approach the work-time hours with at least some amount of detachment.

Ava had blown that intention right out of the water.

Hell, he even grew hard thinking about sex with Ava, and he'd only just come by her hand. She had something with that sending-off stuff. Right now, he could battle anything. Conquer anything. Maybe even write that book.

If rolling around in the oil with Ava wasn't inspirational, he didn't know what was.

He found her snuffing out the candles, the smoke rising above her head. She hadn't yet realized he'd returned, so he stepped back and did what any good reporter did.

He observed.

Her skin still glistened with the oil. He almost hated the idea of Ava stepping below the spray of the water and rinsing all of that away. She'd put her beaded top back on, and was now stuffing the used bags into the trashcan. She was grace and beauty, and any man of any era would want her for his own.

Except him.

Yeah, keep telling yourself that, buddy. You don't want her for your own.

Ava looked up and smiled, surprised to see him.

"Shower's free," he said.

As Ian waited for her, he brainstormed a few possible titles, but gladly put away his pad and pen when he heard her return. He searched her freshly scrubbed face with his gaze. Ava was uncomplicated. Beautiful. No hang-ups.

Who didn't have hang-ups?

"What kind of childhood did you have?" he asked.

"I'll show you." She pivoted on her bare feet and ambled to one of several large bookcases. Her hips rolling slightly as she walked.

He crossed the room to join her at the bookcase. She pulled a photo album from the shelf and flipped through pages until she found a picture of two children with a man and woman in pith hats carrying picks.

"Those are my parents."

"The famous archeologists."

"The very ones."

"I'm guessing the little blonde in pigtails is you."

She nodded. "And that's my little brother, Thad."

He raised an eyebrow. "Thad?"

"Short for Thaddeus. It means praise, and believe me, he's never let us forget it. Our parents named us from the ancient Greek lands where they concentrated their studies."

"And Ava?"

"Like a bird."

His eyes narrowed, as if he were examining her more closely. "I don't think I see that."

She laughed. "It's more in the vein of soaring to greatness."

He smiled. "Ah, I see. How old were you in this picture?"

"Six. That's a site right outside of Athens. Up until I was seven, I didn't know anyplace else but an archeological dig. The summer I turned twelve, I came here, to Oklahoma, to visit my grandma."

"She teach you how to knit? That kind of thing?"

Ava made a snorting sound. "Hardly. Grandma was an actress. In fact, I think an old lover must have left her this place. No, we'd have long drawn-out tea parties, dress up in feather boas and put on elaborate shows."

Ian laughed, imagining the girl she'd been. Then the idea of the woman she was now, prancing in front of him wearing nothing but a boa, chased away everything else.

If it were in the name of research, she'd do it. "Ever think you're still doing pretty much the same thing?"

Now it was Ava's turn to laugh. "You're right. Performing all these rituals in a lot like acting. She must have passed down those interests along with her DNA."

"So, you mentioned a lover."

"Just one of many. She was married four times."

Ian jerked. The lady had his mother beat out by one. But give Janice Cole time.

"Quite scandalous in the 1950s I assure you. Actually, what were my parents thinking? She was no kind of a role model for marital bliss."

Silence stretched between them.

"I was just kidding. She was a great role model. Every one of the men in her life left with a smile."

"I can imagine," Ian said, mentally shrugging off the gloomy thoughts his mother always provoked. "And yet your parents managed to make everything work out long-term."

"Yes, they did. And they were determined to make life a family affair. Despite their obvious displeasure with my chosen career, my parents are wonderful, supportive, but sometimes I wonder, especially after spending so much time with you…"

"Wonder about what?" He'd be happy to indulge her no matter what she had questions about.

She casually lifted a shoulder, but he wasn't fooled. Whatever she planned to reveal was important to her. "On what I may have missed. I want this book to speak to the women of today, but if I'm missing some of those universal experiences, how can we relate? My twenty-first-century dating skills are pretty much worthless. I didn't even know what phone sex was. And sometimes I don't understand the slang you use. We're contemporaries. We're supposed to connect."

"I'd say we connect."

Ava gave him a small shove. "Ian."

"And, it's true, you're far from normal."

She stood to her full height of five foot two. "Now wait a minute, I have done a normal thing or two—"

But Ian gave her a quizzical look. "Never went to a prom. Never cruised. Never hung out at the food court."

"Well—"

"How about a football game? Cheered your team in the rain even though they were losing, because your friends were out there getting their asses handed to them?"

Ava shook her head, closing the picture album and returning it to the bookcase.

"Stayed up past your curfew and gotten grounded?"

Ava folded her arms in front of her chest.

Ian made a tsking sound, his fingers stroking her

cheek. "Like I said, you've missed so much." He met her gaze, then snapped his fingers. "Let's make a deal. By day we work on the book, by night, I'll work on expanding your education."

"Didn't we do that at Club Escape?"

"We're going back to the beginning. First-date kind of stuff. Ava, I'm taking you to high school. Hang on."

In three long strides, Ian was at his laptop and punching something into a search engine.

Then he turned and smiled at her, a smile filled with the kind of excitement that made her yearn to be part of whatever he suggested. She almost gasped. Like he was about to steal her away on an adventure she couldn't wait to take.

"You're in luck. The Pirates are playing their arch rivals the Panthers on the court tonight. And you're going as my date."

She pretended to consider his offer, though she could hardly keep from dancing. "So, is that how boys usually ask for a girl's time?"

Ian winked. "No. I have a lot more finesse now. Be ready in an hour."

THE ROARING NOISE GRABBED her attention first. From the moment Ian held open the glass door leading into the gymnasium, sounds of every kind assailed Ava.

The pounding rhythm from the drums echoed her footsteps, the beat only tempered by the tinny blast of the horns from the high-school band clad in orange T-shirts and jeans. Teenaged girls lined the court wielding large ornamental balls of fluff. The bleachers were filled with cheering crowds clad in orange and black on one side, and patrons sporting the colors of mustard and ketchup on the other. The battle lines were drawn. Tension permeated the scene.

Some version of this scenario played out in cultures around the world and across time. Turf wars or bragging rights, it was all the same. And she couldn't be more excited to be there.

With a whistle and the sound of a buzzer, tall lanky boys streamed onto the hardwood floor, their rubber athletic shoes squeaking.

"Here we go," hollered Ian. He escorted her to an empty spot amongst those proudly wearing the orange and black. "Have you ever seen basketball?"

Ava nodded. "Running up and down. Ball in the net."

Ian's eyes narrowed, but his lips twisted. "Basketball is way more than just running up and down the court. It's the teamwork of passing, the grace of running while dribbling. The excitement of the slam dunk. The refinement of shooting at half court."

She shook her head as if she understood. She pointed to the stands, drawing his attention away from her. "Yeah, the boys with the word *pirate* spelled out on their bare chests in black and orange paint especially demonstrate the grace and refinement of the sport."

Ian shot her a glance, his eyes crinkling at the corners. "Now you've got it."

Ian was back to flirting with her again. Her blood

seemed to heat and thin all at the same time as it rushed through her body.

The buzzer sounded and the players circled their coach while the fluff-brandishing girls took to the court. Loud dance music, similar to what had been playing at Club Escape, blasted over the sound system, and the girls began to move in a coordinated tribal-like dance.

"What is that?" she asked as she pointed.

"Oh, that's the pom squad, and those girls over by the corner are the cheerleaders. They motivate the crowd."

Ava scanned the faces in the bleachers. Every boy had his gaze trained on the dancers now in the middle of the court. "I can see that."

"The pom girls and cheerleaders inspire many fantasies for the adolescent boys. But then in high school, the soccer girls, the tennis girls, the ones who liked drama or sang in choir, they've all starred in one fantasy or another."

"Yours?"

Ian shook his head. "Me? No. I always liked the smart girls with their nose in a book."

Like she'd been. Yeah, now she knew he was flirting. Her pulse picked up its rhythm.

"However, if you did want to wear one of those short pleated shirts, pull your hair into a ponytail and take up some pom-poms, I wouldn't be…turned off."

She laughed, and quelled the urge to remind him that role playing and dress up was quite popular in romantic love play in long-term pair bonds. No, she just laughed and had a good time in Ian's funny teasing presence. She liked this side of him, got the feeling he didn't share it with a lot of people. She was warmed by the thought.

"So, we're at the game. We're having fun. What's next for the typical high-school kids out on a date?" she asked.

A mischievous glint touched his brown eyes. "Let me show you one of my best moves."

Ian stretched, lifted his arms, then casually draped one arm around her shoulder. "Did you catch that?" he asked.

"That fake maneuver to touch me? Yes, I caught that." *Was warmed by it, also.*

"Glad to know I've still got it."

He had something all right.

"Now, as a high-school girl, to show you like me, you—"

"I think I can handle that without instruction. I probably scoot up against you." She slid along the smooth wood of the bleacher seat until their thighs touched. Her skin began to tingle. "Like this."

"Exactly like that."

Okay, this wasn't so different from the things she'd demonstrated at the club. They had pure body alignment. Did he remember what she'd said about body positioning? How it would mirror a man and woman's attunement in bed?

The warmth of his body heated her side. The scent of him filled her nose.

"What do you think?" he asked, his arm drawing her closer to him. Her head resting against his chest. This was a different kind of seduction. Slower. Less combative. She liked it more. That easing into another person.

"The rituals of high school are not so different from other courtship ones. The sponsored gatherings where grown-ups can keep a watchful eye. The couples who try to be close to each other."

"Maybe there is something to that instinct stuff."

She rolled her eyes. "Now what?"

"Well, throughout the evening I see just how low my hand can slip. That's called copping a feel."

Ava turned her head to see his fingers just at the swell of her breast. Her stomach knotted, probably how it would have if they were actually seventeen, in high school, and here in the gym together on a date rather than filling in a gap in her education. "Seeing no luck in any downward direction, what then?"

He sighed heavily, turning his attention back to the action on the court. "I try to actually concentrate on something other than you."

Her whole body warmed at his words. Then her lips twisted in a secret smile. Her instincts were telling her she should make his goal to concentrate on something other than her very, very difficult.

16

AFTER THE PIRATES solidly trounced their rivals, Ian took her on a quick cruise down the famous 39th Street. They stopped at a drive-in for an order of Tater Tots and cherry Cokes.

Ava had been on dates before. An awkward coffee date between classes her freshman year in college. Enthusiastic, yet utterly impersonal dates with story-swapping colleagues. Blind dates set up by her parents with archeologists on dig sites. None of those had felt right. She'd never felt the ease of simply being herself as she did with Ian.

As Ian drove back to Ava's building, they'd talked and laughed and not a single word was about the book. The Bricktown crowd was light that evening, and they didn't have to wait while pedestrians crossed in front of her garage.

Ian pushed the button for the gate to open, then drove the car inside the loading area redesigned to act as a garage. They were acting as if they were a real couple. She liked being with him like this.

Ava reached for her door handle, sad their evening was coming to an end. Not if she could help it.

"Don't go yet," he said, his hand on her shoulder.

He'd turned the car off, but left the music from the radio on. The lights from the dashboard glowed, but didn't fully illuminate his face. She couldn't tell what he was thinking right now.

His fingers curved around her shoulder. "Come closer," he urged, his voice low and seductive. He pulled her as close to his body as the bucket seat would allow.

A small shiver rippled down her back and settled at the base of her spine. "This is called parking, and if I'm lucky, you'll let me get to first base."

"What's first base?"

"It's a baseball term."

She smiled into the night. "Sports. Of course."

"But on a woman, it's this."

Ava's eyes drifted shut as Ian leaned forward. His lips gently brushed hers again. This kiss was different from anything they'd shared before. Slower and yet tentative and less controlled, as if they really were school kids and this was their first kiss.

Then the real Ian, the mature man of the world took over. His mouth teased and tantalized her lips. She sucked in her breath and held it as his mouth opened over hers.

She wound her arms around his neck and curled her fingers into the dark locks behind his ears. The blood zipped through her veins and she released her breath in a sigh.

Ian eased the pressure of his mouth and began to explore the seam of her lips with his tongue. Her breathing came quick and heavy. She opened her lips to him. He groaned and pulled her tighter.

It could have been hours or maybe only a few minutes, but Ian released her, resting his chin on her forehead. His breathing was hard and labored, matching hers.

"So, if that's first base, I take it there is a second?"

"Yes," he told her, his voice strained.

"You up to showing it to me?" she asked, her body on fire with need.

"Believe me when I say I'm up." He swooped in, and gave her another kiss, then his hands slid to her breasts. "That's another move to distract you," he told her. He never dropped his hands.

Her nipples hardened, growing more sensitive against the lace of her bra. "Although I was never your traditional high schooler, I believe I can safely say that the girl wasn't really fooled by your maneuvers."

"And here I was working under this grand illusion all this time." His lips touched hers again, his tongue doing delightful things to her mouth. "My favorite move at the time was the thumb circle."

He circled her breast with his thumb, his rotations getting tighter and tighter until he reached the tip. "If I were feeling bold, I'd move to below her shirt."

Her stomach quivered when she felt his fingertips caress her bare skin.

"I like your bold moves."

"Then check this out," he said. He leaned over and gently sucked her earlobe into his mouth. She felt his hands on her back, then the looseness of her bra.

She moaned as he fully cupped her breasts. "That was some move," she told him.

He chuckled. "Ready for third?"

"There's another base?" she asked, her body beginning to tremble in excitement.

"Oh, yeah."

She almost whimpered as his hands left her breasts. Then she realized their destination. She slid her legs apart as his hands skimmed down her waist, over her hips and to the place between her thighs. She cursed her tight pants for being in the way.

"What I wouldn't have given to touch a girl like you here at seventeen."

"Think of something," she teased.

"I don't know, but I'm feeling the exact same kind of desperation."

She laughed, loved knowing she made him desperate. He rubbed her though her jeans, and suddenly *she* was desperate. His hand created a delicious friction, and she grew warm and wet and ready to take him inside her body.

His lips found hers again, and he kissed her with a hard, passion-filled caress. At the same time, his hand plunged into her jeans under her panties, his fingers discovering her clit.

She pulled her mouth away, moaning. "Ian."

"More? Relax. I want to touch you all over."

"What's the goal of baseball?"

"To hit a home run," he said, his lips lowering to her collarbone.

"What does it mean with a girl. With me?"

He stopped. Glanced at her. "To make love to you."

Her body trembled. She was ready for a home run. "Ian, would you like to come up for some coffee?"

"I can't tell you how much I'd love a cup of coffee."

IT WAS THE QUICKEST he'd ever exited a car. Ian followed her upstairs and into her apartment, nothing and no one around them. They were the only two people in the world. The large front room was still scented by a subtle hint of oil.

Ian locked the door behind them, and trailed her into the kitchen. "Should I actually pretend to make it?" she asked.

A smile briefly touched his lips as he practically stalked toward her. Ava sucked in a breath. The lessons had stopped. Now they were just man and woman. And primal instinct.

He grasped her head, then brought her mouth to his lips. This kiss was neither controlled nor deliberate, but hungry and ready for her.

This was no slow seduction. Only need and passion.

"You on top," she said.

He almost growled. Ian bent, reaching under her knees and hauling her against his body. He marched into her bedroom, and carefully set her on the mattress. He moved to follow her, but she held out her hand.

"Wait," she ordered. "Watch."

She tugged her shirt up and over her head. She'd never bothered to rebutton her jeans after his ministrations in the car, so with a quick flick of her wrist, the zipper was down and her pants off.

She lay against her pillows wearing nothing but a sexy bra and panties. They matched. Black with little pink bows. His new favorite color.

She also hadn't bothered to snap her bra into place after he showed her his moves in conjunction with second base, so the material slipped easily off her body.

She sat before him in only those skimpy little panties. He'd felt what secrets were hidden behind that tiny swatch of lace. She'd described imagining his fingers there, his cock learning those secrets of hers when he'd taught her about phone sex.

What he hadn't done was see her. Her fingers hooked around the edge of her panties, and she slowly wiggled them down her thighs. She kicked them away, and lay before him naked. Availing herself desirably, his arousal grew.

"Ava, here's another conversation you probably need to learn. The condom discussion. Do I need to get them? I have some in my camera bag. But I want you to know that I always play it safe, and I get tested all the time because of my trips overseas. I'm clean."

"Me, too."

He swallowed. "What about pregnancy? You protected there?"

"You don't want to use a condom, do you?"

"I can think of nothing else but the erotic feel of your skin against mine."

"I'm protected there, as well. Don't worry, I won't get pregnant."

He moved toward her, and she put her hand out again. "Wait. Not yet."

He groaned in frustration, but then his eyes widened as she ran her hands down her body to caress her breasts, circle her navel, stroke her clit. His breathing turned shallow and his heart almost went through his ribs at the site of her fingers touching, drawing pleasure, from the very place he wanted to be.

"You like watching me touch myself, don't you, Ian?"

He nodded. "Most men love to see a woman take pleasure in her body. It turns them on, makes them harder."

His cock swelled against his jeans. Quickly he stripped, and her eyes cut his erection a glance. A feminine smile lifted her mouth.

"You see, for men, finding orgasm comes easily. Not so much for women. It takes a little time. Then women discovered the secret, their true power. It's in their pleasure. A man's pleasure, your pleasure is actually heightened by mine."

He nodded, his eyes never leaving the vision of her fingers caressing between her legs.

"That's nature's way of making sure man took care of woman. And if a woman finds a man who's all into taking that time, she knows she has a winner. Nice how it works that way. Look at me, Ian."

His eyes traveled slowly up her body until he met her gaze.

"You're going to make me feel good, aren't you?" she asked, half question, half demand.

"Yes. So good."

She smiled, rested against the pillows and spread her legs for him.

He took himself in hand, moved toward her and found where she'd opened to him. She moaned at the intimate thrust of his flesh sliding into hers.

She locked her legs behind his waist, her body a perfect fit for him. He began to thrust more deeply inside her. Ava started to move with him, against him. Her face tightened. Her muscles gripped him. He ground his hips against hers, finding her clit. That sent her over the edge.

She screamed, her climax hit hard. Her moans, her grip of his penis, it was all too much. He went right over the edge with her.

Soon their breathing returned to normal. The only other sound was the blowers from the heating unit keeping them warm. She lay in his arms, stroking his skin. Utterly content.

Her fingers found the knot of flesh below his right shoulder blade. The scar.

"I was shot."

Ava gasped, her brows knitting together in concern. "Why?"

He shrugged. "Some people don't like reporters."

"So they shot you?"

There were worse things than being shot at, he'd seen plenty of it. Normally, he wouldn't have a problem talking about it. But Ava, as he was quickly realizing, had spent an idealized youth jetting from one remote archeological dig to another, then from the protected walls of university to on-the-job research among cultures that were actually getting along. Not his area of expertise.

Deep down, hell, not so deep down, Ava was an optimist. She easily found the good in anything. Five minutes of hearing his war stories could wipe that brightness of spirit right out.

He sat up, reaching for his shirt.

"Where are you going?"

"Back to the hotel. It's late, I thought you might want your privacy." Plus she hadn't invited him to stay.

"Here's a story you might find interesting. The early American Puritans thought one way to gauge if a couple would be happy together was partly based on whether or not they slept together well."

"Sleep together or actually sleep together?"

She paused for a moment. "Oh, I get it. *Sleep to-gether* is a euphemism for sex. No, in this case, sleeping together actually meant sleeping together. Of course, this was a culture where innocence was valued for both men and women, so a board was placed in the bed between the young man and woman. If they slept well next to each other, it was seen as a good sign."

Ian scrubbed a hand down his face. "Ava, I'm too worn out to work on the book right now."

She shook her head. "What I'm trying to say, and obviously not very well, is that you can stay the night here with me, and I promise—no board."

NATURALLY, HE WOKE WITH her breast in his hand. Was there a better way to sleep? Her soft backside pressed into the heaviness of his erection.

He wound a lazy path with his fingers along her skin, inviting her to wake up. He smoothed the hair back from her neck, watching the blond locks fan out against her pillow. He loved her hair. Loved seeing its softness spread out on the sheets, in his hand, across his body.

With her neck exposed, he ran his tongue along its slope, already knowing that particular spot was one of her favorites.

"Mmm," she moaned and tilted her hips, pushing her soft rear against his hardened cock. She stilled. "Oh."

"Yes, oh."

He lowered his hand until he found her breast again. "I love your breasts. How they respond to me. How you taste."

But as tempting as her breasts may be, he wanted the slick feel of her against his fingers. Ian lowered his hand, stopping as he felt the soft curls between her thighs.

Her hips jerked, forcing her harder against his penis. He fought the urge to sink into her. No, he wanted to touch her, savor her.

He found her clit, damp and so responsive to his touch. She gasped with just his slightest graze. His fingers lowered, and he smiled at what he found. "So warm, so wet. Are you ready for me, Ava?"

She nodded. "Yes."

Ava made a small protesting noise when he moved

his hand away. His fingertips skimmed down her thigh and stopped just above her knee. He pulled her leg over his, getting her into position. His penis found her wet opening, and he slid home. Slowly. They both groaned at the wonderful sensation of her body enveloping his.

His entry complete, his hand sought her clit once more. He stroked her and her every muscle tensed. He thrust and fingered her, every part of his body working together to bring them both pleasure.

Her inner muscles began to quiver around him. He knew she was close. "I want to hear you," he said.

Nothing, not one thing was as erotic as hearing Ava find her release. Her body tensed, then with a burst she clamped down, making him moan.

He doubted he could last much longer. Then he felt her, heard her come. She cried out his name, and he changed his mind. Hearing his name on her lips as she reached her orgasm, now *that* was the most erotic thing he'd ever heard.

"We never really set up any ground rules for what we're doing," she said a few moments later as he was about to drift off to sleep.

"We never really set up any ground rules on who was the decision maker over the book, either, and that's going just fine," he countered.

"A technicality."

Ian rolled onto his back and tucked her head against his chest. "You're going to make me talk, aren't you?"

"You know what I always say—"

"Yes, I know. Most problems between a man and

woman can be cleared up with one good sit-down conversation."

She lifted her head and smiled down at him. "Most conflicts can be avoided that way, too."

He chuckled tiredly. "Doing this after sex is a sneaky blow."

"One practiced by generation after generations of women."

"My job is too complicated for any type of relationship."

"I figured so, like mine. All the traveling. But I like what we have right now."

His heartbeat quickened. "Me, too."

Her eyes narrowed. "And I don't think we need to worry that us making love will ruin the sexual tension of the book. Not anymore."

"So, as long as we're working on the book together…"

He gently pushed her head back down to his chest, her hair fanning across his skin. "Then we're together." He liked the sound of that.

"Why did you become a reporter, Ian?"

Was he off the hook now? No more discussion talk? And why did he feel…let down that she didn't want more of a relationship from him? He sighed heavily. "I've always been curious, always wanted to know what's around the next corner. That first time I was running across the desert with my camera, being chased, that's when I knew who I was. I felt the most alive."

Except right now. Dog-tired, sated and with Ava

lying across his chest, he felt very much alive. They'd said the book, but there was also that vacation. Plus revisions, captions for the photos, suggestions from the copy editor, final proofs…

17

THEIR LAST WEEK had taken on a nice routine of working on the book together in the morning, sending the manuscript pages to his sister in the afternoon and taking pictures at night. They'd made tremendous progress despite being delightfully interrupted to make love and to argue as to who exactly was making the final decisions.

Ian and Ava sat cross-legged on the floor in front of her fireplace as they debated about an ancient warrior class. "I'm telling you it's true."

Ian gave her a skeptical look. "So you're telling me that once they stole the woman and he had her in his possession, it was suddenly okay with her father that she was gone? Her family is hell-bent on protecting her, then all of a sudden all these alpha males just throw up their hands, and say, 'oh, well, you won.'"

Ava made a face. "Well, when you put it like that it does sound far-fetched."

"I think some of your theories need a male's point of view from time to time."

She glanced up sharply. She was about to ask Ian if

he planned to volunteer for the job. As a joke. Then she saw the look on his face. The man was clearly horrified by what had just come out of his mouth.

She searched for something to fill the gulf that suddenly arose between them.

"What I find so interesting," she began, "is that after they've stolen the woman, they then try to woo her. I mean, she's there…he's got her. But he works very hard to win her love."

Ian cleared his throat. "Makes some sense to me. It's not just about sex. He's taken that woman to be his wife. His companion. It's about loneliness, and the need to spend your time with someone who doesn't want to run away or toss a knife in your back."

Silence stretched between them once more. Since they'd become lovers, nothing even close to resembling an awkward moment had passed between them. Now there had been two.

Maybe she should try to tempt him with the paints. Although the idea was to paint yourself and wash your partner, they'd improvised, taking on both roles. She'd try something else. "Maybe he just needed a friend."

"He'd have been insulted if she'd offered. A woman should never tell a man she just wants to be his friend."

"Don't men want friends?"

"Not the women ones," he said drily.

She laughed, and reached for a newspaper clipping. "Hey, I think I found the perfect thing for more of my twenty-first-century dating indoctrination. It's called a cuddle party."

Ian's eyes widened in alarm. "Have you ever been to one? It's supposed to be great. Hugging and touching. Perfect to shake off any intimacy issues."

"I'm fine with my intimacy issues just the way they are."

"You're in a strange mood today."

His eyes narrowed as he looked at her. An odd smile passed across his lips. "You're right." He stood and stretched his legs. "I'm sorry. Miriam e-mailed me and asked for a rush on the last chapter. I stayed up late to finish the manuscript."

"I can't wait to see it, and give you my final decision," she said with a smile. But Ian didn't return her grin at the mention of their inside joke.

"I'll go back to the hotel and print it off."

She glanced down at the case he used to carry his laptop. "Why not print it off here? You can use mine."

Ian shook his head. "I need to call my sister, too."

She rolled to her feet. "In that case, I'll walk you to the door."

He turned toward her, his expression suddenly intense. "Let me take you out to celebrate. Champagne, the works."

"That would be nice."

He kissed her cheek, and shut the door behind him.

Something was wrong, and she had a good idea what it was. The book was complete. A dozen questions swirled around them. The one foremost in her mind... what happened next?

THE PHONE RANG JUST as Jeremy had scooped Miriam against his side. He loved holding her that way. With a reluctant kiss, she slipped out of bed.

She'd been receiving a lot of calls lately, mostly from work. She'd gone in this morning, but had taken the rest of the afternoon off, although a lot of calls were still being diverted her way.

"Hey, Ian."

Jeremy recognized the name. Ian was her brother. The only family she spoke of. He watched as she tucked the phone between her head and shoulder and tugged on a robe. Her long, dark hair looked mussed, and curled down her back. All he could think about was the feel of her hair on his skin.

The soft arousing tickle as it trailed down his stomach as her mouth moved closer to his penis.

He hated that she'd stayed cooped up in her apartment for so long because of him. Miriam was a popular woman. He'd gathered that by the number of phone calls, and the lack of any real substantive food in her kitchen.

"No, I'm not doing anything at all." Her voice carried into the bedroom. Well, they *had* just finished.

He watched as Miriam rolled her head from side to side. "Just a boring weekend at home alone."

Just a boring weekend?

Alone?

His mouth went dry. Something dark and bitter broke free in him. No, when had he become so paranoid? So Miriam wasn't ready to share the news about them with her friends and family. No problem. This was all new to him, too. Except he wanted to shout from the rooftops that Miriam chose to be by his side.

Jeremy thrust the sheets away from his body and swung his legs to the floor. He pulled on his jeans and grabbed his T-shirt. Hating what he was thinking of Miriam.

She said goodbye to her brother and returned to him. "Good news, my brother and the doc finished the book, and if that last chapter is as good as what I've already read, it's going to be great."

He knew how much of her company's resources she'd put behind that book, and its success meant a lot to her both professionally and personally. "Let's go out, Miriam, go to a restaurant and cut loose. Maybe we could invite your friends."

She dropped her hand so fast from around his waist, she almost left skid marks on his back. "No, Jeremy. We can't."

"Can't? What do you mean can't?"

"Going out to a restaurant would be too much like a date. I can't have a relationship with you. Date you. You probably think dating is going to the Taco Barn with change you found between the cushions of your couch. Or on the floorboard of your car."

Jeremy made a face. "That would mean I'd actually have to clean. You're serious? You really don't want to go out? Get to know each other's friends?"

She nodded, her face looking tortured. "Don't you see? I'm over fifteen years older than you, Jeremy. Believe me when I say I can't pass for twenty. Hell, sometimes I can't pass for thirty."

"No one's asking you to pass for anything."

"Do you realize what people will say? They'll take one look at us together and make assumptions. They'll call you my boy toy. I'd look pathetic."

"That's easily fixed. You just stare down anyone who's stupid enough to tell you that and say 'screw you.'"

She stalked into the dining room and huffed, "Oh, that's really mature."

"Then that fits, because apparently I'm low in adult behavior skills."

Miriam twisted her hands together. "Would you stop acting like that?"

He turned a surprised gaze to her. "Like what?"

"Like you're all broken up about this."

The silence between them stretched taut.

She reached for his hand, caught his fingers between hers. "Jeremy, I never meant to hurt you. I didn't ask you to come here. You did that all on your own. I never even returned your phone calls."

His hands dropped to his sides, and he took a step back. He could accept a woman not interested in him. He was a guy who could bow out gracefully. But with Miriam, he'd planned to at least put up a fight. A fight she apparently didn't want him to make.

"If you'd turned me down right from the beginning, offered to play hostess to me being tourist, instead of us winding up in bed—I would have walked on. That would have been the end of it."

Her brown eyes didn't soften.

"But the minute you fell into my arms, the second

your lips touched mine, I knew what that kick in the stomach was all about. What I'd been missing since you left Oklahoma."

Miriam refused to meet his eyes.

"A fire burns between us." He grabbed her shoulders. "If this were no more than a second one-night stand, it would have been through by the weekend. You wouldn't have extended it into this week. It's hotter than it was before."

"Think of this as just getting lucky. You're twenty. You should be into easy lays."

He shook his head. "Don't make this into that…"

"I did. Our time—"

"Our time was all about you and me. It's been there all along. And for the record, I could afford to take you someplace other than Taco Barn. I have a good job back home."

Her eyes narrowed, finally meeting his gaze. "One that allows you to take off and leave for weeks at a time?" she asked. Her voice skeptical.

"As a matter of fact, yes. I own my own business. I flip houses. I buy them cheap, fix them up and sell them at a nice profit. The housing market is usually slower in February. That's when I normally book my vacation. And don't worry, even if I should lose a job, I can always find another. People are always looking for someone who can fix things. I can go anywhere I want. Men who can work with their hands, cabinetry, plumbing, we're a dying breed."

"Oh," Miriam said, suddenly feeling deflated. She'd insulted Jeremy. "I'm sor…"

Her words trailed off as he brushed a stray lock of hair from her face and tucked it behind her ear. "Don't be too hard on yourself, though. You spent this time with me because you love me."

She jerked away. "Jeremy, don't make this into something it's not. I know you expect to have what your parents had. To fall instantly in love and live happily forever. But they were lucky. It doesn't work like that for everyone. For most people."

"My parents listened to their hearts. And it wasn't just luck. They worked at their marriage. They *made* it work. They became the person the other one could count on. I want you to count on me. I want to be the man who left the world a little better than the way I found it by fixing things with my hands. I want to be the guy who took his kids out for doughnuts on a Saturday morning so Mommy could sleep in. But one thing I don't want to be—the man whose woman was too embarrassed to introduce him to her friends."

She stood away from him. "You don't love me, and I certainly don't love you," she told him.

"Prove it," he challenged.

You went to bed with me because you love me, she answered, but didn't say the words out loud.

Jeremy stepped toward her. "Tell me how you feel about me. Tell me you don't love me."

"I don't love you," she told him quickly. Firmly.

She saw that flicker of hurt touch his eyes. She knew

better than this. At least she should have. She was older and supposedly wiser. Miriam had spotted the vulnerability in him. She should have known it would come to this, and avoided it. The responsibility of hurting him cut deeply, she was sick and angry with herself.

"That sounded really convincing."

"The truth usually is."

"Prove it's the truth."

She tilted her head toward him. "How?"

He held out his arms. "Come over here and kiss me."

Sexier words had never been spoken. Desire pounded her body. "I'm not going to kiss you." But her words lacked any defiant conviction.

"Well, how do I know that's how you really feel?"

"I just told you how I really feel."

She couldn't take much more of this. She'd kiss him, prove him wrong, send him back to Oklahoma. And she'd make a vow. Never, ever get involved with someone under thirty. Forty.

"No sly stuff."

"You assuming you're going to lose?"

"No, I'm assuming that you're tricky."

"Tricky? I'm hurt you'd say that. I've always been straightforward with you. I want you. I want to spend more time with you, and get to know you even better. It's you who hasn't been honest. With yourself."

"Oh, come over here, kiss me and get it over with."

"Now darlin', I can say I've had better offers than that."

"Fine." Anything to get this point proven and the whole thing over with.

She walked with slow, deliberate steps toward him. He took a seat at her dining-room table.

So her younger lover wasn't going to make this any easier for her. She had no desire to hurt him. She wouldn't try to lay on him a kiss that would send Jeremy reeling. She'd simply give him his kiss, all the while remaining detached.

After Oklahoma, he'd haunted her nights, but now that was over. She just had to make him believe it. And herself. She'd focus on something completely mundane, *not* on the sexy ruggedness of his voice.

She lowered her head, and her hair fell forward, shrouding them. At the first touch, his lips remained firm. And closed. Miriam pulled away slightly and darted her tongue along the seam of his lips, then traced the outer edges with the tip of her tongue.

Still nothing from him.

The blood pounded in her ears, her mouth grew desperate for the taste of him.

"What are you trying to do here? Why aren't you kissing me back?"

"Maybe if you put some feeling into it. If you trusted yourself to," his voice taunted.

"Maybe it's because there are no feelings involved."

"Then prove it, and kiss me like you mean it."

Miriam braced her arms on the armrests of her very expensive mahogany dining-room chair. She felt like rolling up her sleeves and getting to work on this guy. She trailed small kisses to his ear then licked the sensitive skin below.

He sucked in a breath.

Good. She traced the edge of his ear with her tongue. Jeremy moved his hands to her head and tugged her face to his. He met her lips with his mouth open. Fire shot through her body, tightening her nipples and sending a rush of feeling downward, fueling her desire.

Jeremy jerked her closer, his kiss deepening.

Off balance, she fell onto his lap, straddling his legs. The hard ridge of his cock sent another wave of warmth through her. She pushed herself closer, touching him through their scant clothes. She began to move up and down, mimicking the moves she'd make on the mattress.

Jeremy placed his hands on either side of her face and gently thrust her away. She balanced her forehead on his. Their heavy breathing filled the room. Jarringly, she sat up and shoved the hair from her face. She couldn't pretend that was nothing—her nipples still throbbed.

Okay, it was sex. Just sex. But nothing else.

Through a sensual haze, their gazes locked. His eyes blazed like sunlit sapphires.

"You're right," he said, his tone flat. His expression blank. "You don't love me."

He'd called her bluff.

And then Jeremy Kelso pushed himself up from the chair, collected his things and walked out her door and out of her life.

That's when she noticed the light in her kitchen was working.

18

Ian looked at his watch for the third time. A feeling completely foreign and strange came over him. He wasn't exactly sure what it was until he looked at his watch yet again in the span of less than thirty seconds. That's when the feeling wagged its smug little finger at him.

He was nervous.

Why was he nervous? He wasn't a nervous kind of guy. People shot at him, and he didn't blink at that.

But he knew the reason. He was edgy because his time with Ava was over. He'd typed the last word of the book last night. This morning he'd scanned the last picture and e-mailed everything to his sister. He expected to hear from her at any moment. But he wasn't worried about her thoughts on the book. He knew that *Sex by the Book*—the new title—was stunning. Ava had created something amazing. But...

He'd faced guns, angry officers of the law and death, but none of that compared with facing Ava when she arrived. He'd said goodbye to a few women in his day, but they'd all been like him, looking for some contemporary company.

And he'd never been in love with any of them.

In fact, falling in love had never entered his mind. *What the hell?*

Had the word *love* just charged into his head? Twice? If it had, he planned to make it exit. Love, if he even believed it existed, didn't mix with anyone with the last name Cole.

But then he thought of the beautiful woman on her way to him. Damn. He'd done it. Or she'd done it. Whoever it was, he'd fallen in love with Ava Simms.

He'd been an idiot not to see it coming. How could he not spend all that time with someone as witty, smart and sexy as Ava and not fall in love with her?

Yes, it was definitely time to go.

Then he saw her walk through the door of the elegant restaurant where he'd booked a table for them to celebrate the completion of the book. Huge chandeliers hung from the ceiling, and the most expensive china and silverware graced the table.

The perfect setting for a breakup.

She smiled at the hostess in greeting. He'd miss that smile aimed in his direction, Ava's blond hair flowing freely around her face the way he liked. Damn, she was so beautiful. And challenging. She made him wish for things. Things he could never have.

It was right to end it now.

Ava removed her sunglasses and he watched as her beautiful green eyes scanned the area. Their gazes met. Held.

Those emerald eyes of hers communicated a wealth

of feeling. Each intriguing. But the emotion that called to him, drew him in, was the promise he saw lingering in their lush depths. A promise he couldn't take her up on.

She smiled at him now, and he almost changed his mind. Almost. He didn't return her smile.

Ava slid into the plush seat across from him, her eyes searching his. She seemed to find what she was looking for because she dropped her gaze and sighed. "You're leaving, aren't you?"

He nodded.

"What about taking a vacation?"

"You know that wasn't really real. We just told ourselves that. My flight leaves tonight."

A line formed between her eyebrows. "So soon? Don't I get any say in this?"

He shrugged, knowing he was hurting her. "Why would you?" he asked, angry at himself for being deliberately cruel.

He sighed and looked around the restaurant, avoiding looking at her. Having this last meal with her had been a mistake. Soon she'd have him rethinking his decision to leave. To follow his chosen career path. Like after the sending-off ceremony, when he thought he could do anything.

She lifted her shoulders in a slight shrug. "Yeah, why would I?"

A waiter approached their table. Oblivious to the tension between them, he asked merrily, "What can I get you folks to drink?"

Her green eyes examined Ian once more, then she

looked up toward their waiter and offered him a tight smile. "Nothing for me, thanks. I've decided I'm not hungry."

She stood, and Ian stood along with her. "Ava, let's—"

"No, Ian, it's okay. Stay, or go. It doesn't matter. I'll take a walk around the canal. Plan what I'm going to do next. Maybe sort out that vacation."

He flinched. The idea of her vacationing, having a life without him, made him ache.

"In fact, I missed a call from your sister." Ava balanced on her tiptoe and kissed his cheek. "Take care," she whispered below his ear.

This wasn't right. She shouldn't be leaving him. He shouldn't be letting her go. Letting her go? Hell, he'd pushed her away.

They should be celebrating over wine and candles and all that romantic stuff he knew would make her happy. They should be swapping memories of the last few days of the writing process. Laughing over times they'd argued, because it was done now and the finished product really worked.

Afterward, he would take her into his arms. Lead her onto the dance floor, then later hold her in his arms while they made love. Any normal boyfriend should be thrilled things were beginning to work out for her career.

But he wasn't boyfriend material. His sister called him an adrenaline junkie. A risk taker. And there was Ava, a gentle researcher. An academic. How would their lives ever meet?

Ending this—it was the right thing to do. He knew it. But knowing that didn't make it stop hurting like hell.

MIRIAM SAT FOR A moment and watched the blinking cursor on her laptop screen. It felt good to be back in the swing of things. She knew catching up on work at home would make her return that much smoother.

Work. The one thing that was always there for you. Never left your side.

She'd learned on her father's knee that reaching the top level of a chosen career was the epitome of success. Things like family and kids never really factored in. Certainly hadn't played a key role with her dad, anyway.

Words like *kids,* and *mommy* and *doughnut* seemed to roll off Jeremy's tongue without him even choking. Weird.

Miriam rubbed her temples. She couldn't remember the last time she let someone else handle the particulars. Jeremy had wanted to handle the particulars. He'd been interested in her business. Keeping their home clean. Feeding her. Fixing the things that were broken in her life.

But she'd realized a long time ago, there was no fixing some things that were broken. Especially when the breaks and tears had happened so long ago. She'd been cynical about love, about men, about relationships by the time she was thirteen. A few delightful days spent with Jeremy were never going to fix that.

Yet…she'd wanted them to.

A knock sounded at her door and she jumped, knowing it was him. It had been two long days since Jeremy had left her apartment. Left her.

But she'd recognized his knock. A funny thing to be familiar with, but there it was. She could distinguish his knock as surely as she could make out his scent or the build of his body.

She raced for the door, swinging it open. Jeremy stood there, looking sad and oh, so good on her eyes. "I'm leaving tonight. Thought I'd say goodbye."

She nodded, not really trusting herself to speak.

He rubbed the calloused pad of his thumb against the swollen softness of her lips. She darted out a tongue and tasted his skin, unable to stop herself. With a groan, his lips found hers with an urgency that made her heart skip and her toes curl.

She buried her fingers in Jeremy's hair, pulling him closer as she opened her mouth for him.

Thrills shot through her as his tongue entered her mouth and filled her with heat. Jeremy's hands moved from her waist to cup her breasts, and she moaned deep in her throat.

MIRIAM SMOOTHED HER HAIR from her forehead and molded herself to Jeremy, not ready to let go of him yet. She placed a kiss in that sensitive place between his neck and shoulder. "I'm glad you came back."

Jeremy lifted from her, his expression…not one that was typical of Jeremy. "Yeah, me, too," he said as he rolled off her.

Miriam scooted up against the headboard, watching as he reached for his jeans and stepped into them. He'd just tugged his shirt over his head when she finally clued in to the fact that he was actually getting dressed. Dressed to leave her.

"Are you going?" she asked. Surprised.

He gave her a tight nod. "It's time."

She yanked the sheet up and around her body. "Oh, well, you can…" Her words trailed off. What was she about to offer? That he could stay with her? Until when, morning? She recalled supervising the article on women broadcasting mixed signals.

What kind of mixed signals was she disseminating to Jeremy?

That she wanted him?

That she only wanted him for sex?

That she'd only use him for sex because she was afraid of what others would say and think?

When had she become so shallow? When had she become so much like her mother?

Her eyes prickled, and the back of her throat tightened. What a cold bitch she was.

"You came back tonight to show me how I made you feel. To show me what it feels like to only be used for sex."

His sad blue eyes met hers, and he shrugged. "I started out that way, but I could never use you for sex, Miriam. I care for you too much."

Was she so shallow she was about to lose the best thing in her life?

No.

She didn't deserve him.

He tugged on a boot. She didn't deserve him, but she wasn't so stupid she was going to let him walk out of her life so easily. Things seemed so clear now. Sure, the cynical side of herself would say she was trying to pound square pegs into round holes because she wanted Jeremy.

And so what if she were? Wasn't he, wasn't the thing between them worth fighting for?

"Jeremy, wait."

He turned slowly, reluctantly.

Her stomach clenched. She'd never seen that look on his face. Dejected. Tired. Resolved. "There are a million reasons why this shouldn't work between us."

"You've told me already."

"But I haven't told you why it can."

The next words would be hard to get out. She hadn't said them to another person since she was seven.

"I love you. You were right. I don't know how it happened, maybe that scientist author who's working with my brother is right, and something in you triggered something in me."

She wrapped her fingers around his hand. "I know you'd never hurt me. You'll try to rescue me and take care of me, and I'll just say 'screw it' to anyone who says something about our age difference."

Miriam saw his body tense. Then relax. In relief she realized she was winning him.

His expression lightened. "That's my Miriam."

She reached for him, drew him to her. "That's who I'll be. Your Miriam."

He lowered his head and kissed her gently on the lips.

"I have tickets to the ballet tomorrow. I can't wait to introduce you to my friends," she said.

"Ballet? How about a baseball game? Maybe even tennis? I'll even throw in dinner."

She let out a laugh, and his grin turned into a full smile.

"Tough," she said and touched the tip of her tongue to the seam of his lips.

"Miriam, when you do things like that to me, I can't go slow."

She ran her tongue up the side of his neck until she found his ear, tugging his lobe gently with her teeth.

Jeremy scooped her up in his arms. "I'll wait for slow next time. I want you now."

Miriam liked the sound of that.

AVA STOOD IN THE OPEN doorway of her apartment, only to find Ian leaving a stack of papers she assumed was the last chapter of the manuscript. He dropped the spare key she'd given him on top. She was startled, but not entirely surprised to see him still there. Something between them felt…unfinished. At least in her mind. Perhaps he felt it, too.

He stood slowly and faced her. "Miriam approved the book, it's going into production."

She forced a smile, feeling next to nothing. "That's great."

"You should be getting the rest of your advance now. That should seed you for your next project or your vacation."

"Actually, I pitched another idea to Miriam. It came to me on my walk."

He stuffed one hand into the back pocket of his jeans. "Really? I thought you might try to find work teaching."

"I thought I would, too. But now I find I'm missing doing the actual field research. I think I'd much rather be out discovering new things than writing about them. It was a large part of my life, and I want to get back to it. Like you and being a reporter."

He nodded slowly. "Just like me."

"In fact, something you said gave me the idea. Remember how you said I knew all these ancient customs, but nothing of my own? Well, that's what I plan to work on, the more unusual marriage and courtship customs found in modern times."

"Where do you plan to go first?"

"Miriam and I agreed on Sweden. I want to explore the rituals from colder climates. See how they're different. How they're the same. There's something kind of sexy about spending months indoors under the covers with your love." Her voice trembled. She'd tried to make it detached, but all she could imagine was snuggling under the covers with Ian.

"Maybe when you're done with the research on that we could…" His words trailed.

Her throat began to ache. He was going to say work on the book together. "Yeah. Maybe. I'd like that." She paused. Somehow this conversation felt like that coffee role play. She'd offer him coffee. He'd accept knowing she was inviting him in for something other than a hot beverage.

Except this time it was about something a lot more

close to her than coffee. This was the role play about not seeing each other again, while pretending they would. This role play only made her sad.

"Where are you headed?" she asked.

"The jungles of South America. Some interesting stuff brewing down there."

She suppressed a shudder at the thought of Ian in the line of fire. "I'm sure you'll enjoy the pace."

A long awkward silence followed. She should be used to those by now, but she wasn't. Ava folded her arms across her chest. He lifted the strap of his laptop case over his shoulder.

"You know, there's one thing you never talked to me about twenty-first-century dating."

"What's that?"

"How to act when it ends."

Something dark and fierce blazed in Ian's brown eyes, then faded. His fingers lifted, almost as if he were going to reach for her. But he didn't.

"It ends as friends."

Her heart ached. She didn't want friendship. She wanted more. "I thought you told me men never wanted friendship from a woman."

Ian shrugged, and dropped his gaze. "Sometimes when that's all you can have, that's what you take."

Her throat tightened. "Ian, I wanted to thank you for everything. If you hadn't—"

He shook his head, and his eyes met hers once more. "No need to thank me. It was all you. I just helped you...bring it out."

Ian smiled then, the first genuine smile he'd given her since the end of the book. "Goodbye, Ava."

Two Weeks Later

"PEOPLE AS HAPPY AS you are shouldn't be allowed in public," Ian said, as he cradled his head in his hands.

Miriam patted him on the shoulder. "And someone as miserable as you are should be shot and put out of their misery. What is wrong with you? I thought you'd be happy covering those peace talks. They're not very peaceful, are they? That's right up your alley."

"I was. Am."

"Come on, baby brother. Tell me what it is."

"Drifting from one place to another isn't exciting anymore. I don't get the rush. That jolt of excitement. Chasing danger just feels...silly." Because nothing could ever be as thrilling and challenging as Ava.

"What is it you've been chasing all this time, Ian?"

He lifted his shoulders. "I don't know. I don't know if I ever did know."

"Now you seem more like you're running."

And how. But what was he running from? From Ava? From his feelings? What if he did find her again? Try for something resembling a normal relationship? Things would eventually fall apart around him. They always did. And then he'd hurt like hell.

He was hurting right now.

At least if he found her again, he'd get to spend the good times with her while it lasted, right?

"Sis, we're in the media biz. Love and happiness, it's all an illusion. Our job is to market happiness, but promote it in such a way that people always want more. We sell a fantasy. How do you know if you're really in love?"

Miriam rolled her eyes. "You know what not being in love feels like, right? Do you feel like that?"

"No." He didn't have the strength to deny it any longer. It was time to face facts. Weeks had passed, and whatever trick passion played on his heart had not faded. Usually he forgot the woman as soon as they'd both said goodbye.

He *was* in love with Ava.

A slight smile tugged at his lip. "What's even more bizarre, I was actually happy with Ava." He knew some people who, when they found their latest "love of their life," became miserable and made everyone around them unhappy, too.

"What's more, you're not happy now without her," Miriam pointed out.

He scrubbed a hand down his face. "You're right, but you know how things are. How could I subject her to me? She's really bett—"

"If you actually say something stupid like 'she's better off without me' and you're backing away to be good to her, I'm really going to scream."

"Look at Mom, Dad. They probably passed along some personality trait that actually makes the person I love better off not being around me. They were bad enough as single entities, but combined together in my DNA…"

"The love-destruction gene? I don't think so." Miriam's lips firmed. "I almost pushed away the best thing that's ever come into my life because I was afraid I was too much like Dad, enjoying a trophy boy toy. You're worried you're like Mom. Are you using Ava to your own selfish advantage? Only being with her because of what she can give you before you move on?"

He shook his head. "No."

"Then what's the problem? The fact that you're willing to push her away, wrong though it is, proves you're looking out for her best interest, and not being a jerk. And screw Mom and Dad as examples. If anything, I think we're better candidates for marriage because we've witnessed firsthand all the things you can do wrong to ruin a relationship."

The tension he'd been carrying in his shoulders, and the ache twisting his gut relaxed. "Right. Who we should be feeling sorry for are all those people who grew up in normal, functional homes and think love is easy."

Brown eyes met brown eyes and they both laughed.

"I do love Ava, and you know, when I was with her I never felt that urge to keep looking over the next hill to see if there was something more exciting."

"Isn't there someone else you should be saying all this to?"

Ian looked up and met his sister's serious gaze.

"You're happy? You really are?"

Miriam nodded.

"I'm out of here."

Miriam reached over and buzzed Rich through the intercom. "Book Ian on a flight to Sweden."

AVA PULLED ON ANOTHER pair of thermal underwear before sitting cross-legged on her bed. Who knew sleeping on a bed made of snow and ice would actually be comfortable? But it was. Everything about the ice hotel was amazing.

She'd lived all over the world, seen a lot of hotels, motels and patches of dirt on the ground, but she'd never slept in a place like this. A hotel in the village of Jukkasjärvi made entirely from the frozen water of the nearby Torne River. She'd loved this amazing structure the moment she'd stepped out of the cold into the warmer reservation area of the hotel. Warmer, but not warm. She appreciated the snowcoat, hat and mittens provided by the hotel, and was glad she'd packed so much thermal underwear.

This clothing was certainly different from the attire worn by the cultures she usually researched. The coat might not show a woman's form to its best advantage, but the women of the Artic region still kept their beds warmed at night with the presence of a man when desired. She was looking forward to learning the flirting techniques these women utilized while freezing their backsides off and in the bulkiest clothing ever created.

Maybe it had something to do with the saunas. The Swedes took steam to a whole new level, and she never realized how much she'd enjoy the ice sauna in the hotel. Relaxing in the outdoor hot tub while staring up at the designs the Northern Lights created in the night sky was a nice backdrop for a romantic interlude.

She snapped a few pictures of the interior of her room,

the large blocks of ice carved in a gothic style. Each room of the hotel was a work of art, the architecture unique, and she'd stayed in four different quarters so far. The clearness of the ice cast a beautiful light blue hue, and the beauty of the ice sculptures made her forget the cold.

Made her forget almost everything but Ian.

Ava pulled the blanket from the bed and wrapped it around her shoulders. The window beckoned her, as it did whenever she was alone in here. She faced to the left. That was the right direction for South America, right?

She sighed heavily. Maybe she'd messed up there that last day with Ian. Maybe she shouldn't have taken his word for it, as friends. Maybe she should have fought for what she knew he felt for her. He had felt something, she knew it.

Or maybe it was this beautiful, magical place making her get all fanciful about Ian. This hotel that made her feel as if she was living the life of a fairy-tale ice princess waiting for her misguided prince to wise up.

The hotel would be gone soon. Already she heard the faint drip of the melting ice. Spring would come and begin to claim her room, by summer it would all be gone. Only to be reborn in the fall. A new hotel would be carved from the ice. A new vision.

Ava knew there was probably a metaphor about her relationship there. She'd explore it right now but she had a wedding to take part in. No longer was she just an observer: Ava Simms was living life now. She tossed off the blanket and headed for the door.

She found the excited bride, Penny, waiting for her,

already dressed in a medieval gown of lace, her hair tied with garland.

"I can't wait until your book comes out. Can you see what's in my hair? Gavin liked the story you told last night so much, he tied it himself. The flowers were going to be for my bouquet, but who cares? What's a few less blooms?"

Take that, Ian Cole. "You look lovely, and I have something for your bouquet." Ava opened a small plastic bag, and pulled out some greenery.

The bride caught the strong aroma. "That smells."

"I know, and for good reason. The ancients of this land believed small trolls and evil gnomes would plague young couples. But there was a remedy."

Penny made a face. "I'm guessing that the remedy is what smells."

"You guessed right. The bride and her attendants are to carry herbs and stinking weeds, but I think the gnomes and trolls can be successfully chased away with just a bit tucked into your bouquet."

After a quick hug, they both made their way to the ice church. Ava took a seat and noted the beautifully designed space with arches and an ice altar carved with intricate designs.

The ceremony was beautiful, and it wasn't the first time she wondered about what Ian's reactions would be to all she'd found here. What would he think of the ceremony? Which customs would he want to recreate with her?

About every fifteen seconds she thought of something she wanted to tell him. Whenever she spotted something new, she immediately thought of sharing it with him. When had she ever wanted to share her work with anyone before?

Only with Ian.

Now, for the first time she understood her parents' need to work together.

The happy couple was headed for the ice bar for a celebratory drink, and she was invited. Although the heavy coats were still needed, the large room was a favorite place for all the hotel guests to mingle. The blue lights of the bar reminded Ava of her first experience of a club scene with Ian, although the elegance of the large bar crafted entirely from ice and the drinks served from ice glasses was about as far removed from the experience as Oklahoma was from Sweden.

Which was why she was so surprised to see someone else completely out of place.

"Ian?" she called, unable to hide her shock, her heart pounding from the surprise of seeing him.

She watched him tense as he looked her way. That familiar tight ache she felt in her throat whenever she thought of him slammed into her with a vengeance. A million questions appeared and evaporated in her mind.

He was at her side in five long strides. "What are you doing here?" she asked. "Is there something wrong with the book?"

Ian shook his head. "I came for you."

She blinked. "But what about those things you said?

You're the risk taker. How you live to be in the danger zone, and there's no place for—"

He grasped her hands. Were his hands actually shaking? "I don't need that rush anymore. I've discovered a way to feel alive without risking my neck."

She forced herself to be still. Stay calm. Don't give in to the hope. "What's that?"

"Being with you. I love you, Ava."

She closed her eyes tightly as he spoke, savoring his words.

"I've been miserable without you."

His fingers curled around her chin and her lids opened. His smile wasn't as bright. His eyes no longer so hopeful. "Do you need help with how a twenty-first-century woman responds to a man who tells her he loves her?"

She shook her head. "No, I think I have that covered. I love you, too."

He hauled her to his chest, his strong arms surrounding her. Making her feel loved. She glanced up at him. "But where will you work? What will you do?"

"Don't worry about it. In fact, I think I found the perfect setting for my next assignment."

"Where?"

"Anywhere you are, if that works for you. This cold, beautiful place is the perfect setting for a project I had in mind. I've come to really enjoy exploring cultures and documenting courtship rituals. Together. If you want me."

"Well, I don't know about that," she said, her voice taking on a teasing quality. "I think we're going to have to discuss this decision-making process. Set down some ground rules. You know what ground rules are?"

His lips twisted. "I'm familiar with the concept."

"In fact, we can settle this the old-fashioned way. The Swedes have a very interesting custom. Instead of the father giving his daughter away, the bride and groom arrive at the church together. Whoever enters first, that's the person who'll be the decision maker."

"The chapel down that hallway?" he asked.

"Yes."

"Hey," she called, when all she could see was Ian's retreating back. He was trying to get a head start. The cheater.

"You know it won't count because we haven't filled out any of the paperwork," she said when she caught up to him at the entrance of the ice chapel.

Ian looked at Ava and smiled. "Always trying to catch me on a technicality…and I wouldn't have it any other way."

Then he reached for her and brought her into his arms and they crossed the threshold into the church together.

Silhouette® Desire

NEW YORK TIMES BESTSELLING AUTHOR

DIANA PALMER

A brand-new Long, Tall Texans novel

IRON COWBOY

*Available March 2008
wherever you buy books.*

Private jets. Luxury cars. Exclusive five-star hotels.
Designer outfits for every occasion and an entourage
to see to your every whim...

In this brand-new collection,
ordinary women step into the
world of the super-rich and are

TAKEN BY
THE MILLIONAIRE

Don't miss the glamorous collection:
MISTRESS TO THE TYCOON
by **NICOLA MARSH**

AT THE BILLIONAIRE'S BIDDING
by **TRISH WYLIE**

THE MILLIONAIRE'S
BLACKMAIL BARGAIN
by **HEIDI RICE**

HIRED FOR THE BOSS'S BED
by **ROBYN GRADY**

Available March 11
wherever books are sold.

$1.00 OFF

The bestselling Lakeshore Chronicles continue with *Snowfall at Willow Lake*, a story of what comes after a woman survives an unspeakable horror and finds her way home, to healing and redemption and a new chance at happiness.

SUSAN WIGGS

NEW YORK TIMES BESTSELLING AUTHOR

SUSAN WIGGS

"Susan Wiggs's novels are beautiful, tender and wise."
—Luanne Rice

Snowfall at Willow Lake
The Lakeshore Chronicles

On sale February 2008!

SAVE $1.00

off the purchase price of **SNOWFALL AT WILLOW LAKE** by Susan Wiggs.

Offer valid from February 1, 2008, to April 30, 2008.
Redeemable at participating retail outlets. Limit one coupon per purchase.

52608168

5 65373 00076 2   (8100) 0 11463

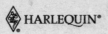

HARLEQUIN®

Blaze™

COMING NEXT MONTH

#381 GETTING LUCKY Joanne Rock
Blush

Sports agent Dex Brantley used to be the luckiest man alive. But since rumors of a family curse floated to the surface, he's been on a losing streak. To reverse that, he hooks up again with sexy psychic Lara Wyland. Before long he's lucky in a whole new way!

#382 SHAKEN AND STIRRED Kathleen O'Reilly
Those Sexy O'Sullivans, Bk. 1

When Gabe O'Sullivan describes his friend Tessa Hart as a work in progress, it gets Tessa to thinking. She's carried a torch for Gabe forever, but maybe now's the time to light the first spark and show him who's really ready to take their sexy flirting to the next level!

#383 OFF LIMITS Jordan Summers

Love happens when you least expect it. Especially on an airplane between Delaney Carter, an undercover ATF agent, and Jack Gordon, a former arms dealer. With their lives on the line, can they find a way to trust each other… once they're out of bed?

#384 BEYOND HIS CONTROL Stephanie Tyler

A reunion rescue mission turns life-threatening just as navy SEAL Justin Brandt realizes he's saving former high school flame Ava Turkowski. Talk about a blast from the past…

#385 WHAT HAPPENED IN VEGAS… Wendy Etherington

For Jacinda Barrett, leaving Las Vegas meant leaving behind her exotic dancer self. Now she's respectable…in every way. Then Gideon Nash—her weekend-she'll-never-forget hottie—shows up. Suddenly she's got the urge to lose the clothes…and the respectability!

#386 COMING SOON Jo Leigh
Do Not Disturb

Concierge Mia Traverse discovers a body in the romantic Hush hotel, which is booked for a movie shoot. Detective Bax Milligan is assigned to investigate and keep Mia under wraps. Hiding out with her in a sexy suite is perfect—except for *who* and *what* is coming next.…

HBCNM0208